JANUS UNFOLDING

The Urritan Legacy

C. A. KNUTSEN

BOOK FIVE OF THE JANUS UNFOLDING SERIES

Acknowledgements

I would like to thank Judy Knutsen, Kenneth Kussmann, and Russel Beard for their thorough reading of a proof copy and their feedback.

caknutsen.com

Copyright © 2019 C. A. KNUTSEN
All Rights Reserved

Cover Art: Jeff Brown Graphics

ISBN - 13: 978-1-7330003-2-1

Janus Unfolding Books

Emergence

Factotum

Inheritance

Ancient Agendas

The Urritan Legacy

Contents

Concepts and Characters

H1 - Humans with standard Homo Sapiens DNA

H2 - Starting in the year 2000 some Human beings were born with a more complex DNA. The number of H2s in the population increased rapidly. By 2050 it was clear that H2s were not aging as fast as H1s.

Sam Baxter, Compass Enterprises, and Sunaj (Soon'-ahj) - Sam was born an H2 in the year 2000. Sam founded Compass Enterprises, headquartered in Seattle, Washington, and the H2 scientific research organization, Sunaj, which he located near the town of Frazier in Southwest Washington.

Martha - The cyber-based intelligence (she doesn't like the title "artificial intelligence") that emerged from complex systems developed by Sam. Martha made a copy of herself named Athena.

Janus (Jann'-us) - In 2051 the population of H2s on Earth was 250 million. H2s were just beginning to use telepathy to contact each other. It was at this point that the heightened conscious activity among the H2s triggered the awakening of a global consciousness, which became Janus, a being unto itself.

The Planet Ocean, the Cheneshi (Chen'-esh-ee)**, and Sways** – The H2s on Earth received a telepathic message from a planet fifty light-years away. Those sending the message were tree-like creatures called Cheneshi. They lived below the surface of their ocean. The Cheneshi had a problem and were reaching out to Earth for help. Among all the Cheneshi, Sways became the scientist's primary contact.

Jesse Chavez - Jesse was among the first two hundred H2s found by Sam Baxter. Jesse led the team of scientists going to Ocean.

Carmen Willathorpe - An anthropologist by training. After an accident on Ocean, Carmen learned that she could sense consciousness of other sentient beings at enormous distances.

Lorengi (Lor-n-gee'), **Ahleeto** (Ah-lee-tow'), **and Thelika** (Thel-ee-ka') – **a Lorengi Ship** - While on Ocean, the Sunaj scientists found a facility that had been constructed on an island by a race called the Lorengi. Ahleeto, a former Lorengi leader had stored herself digitally in the facility and presented herself in holographic form. She introduced the Humans to Thelika. Lorengi ships like Thelika were sentient beings grown by the Lorengi. Thelika and the other Lorengi ships were telepathic, and also could teleport across vast interstellar spaces. Ahleeto had lost contact with her people thousands of years earlier. They were found and rescued later with the help of Carmen and the others. The Lorengi had learned that they were dying as a race and had chosen to store themselves digitally as Ahleeto had, and all resided on one enormous Lorengi vessel.

Annli (Ahn'-lee) - An ancient race that had transformed into pure energy. The individuals were separate energy beings which could communicate telepathically with others. **Theron -** an Annli individual which had been selected to work with Sam Baxter and his team.

The Urritan Legacy

Human
> Kristen Rodgers – Director of Compass Enterprises
> Thornton Rodgers – Engineer at Compass
> Travis Beckwith – Director of Nano Group at Sunaj

On Planet Agar (Perillian)
> Agar (A'- gar) – the AI managing Perillian
> Johar (Jo' R) – Agara village leader
> Sela (See' la) – Agara village person

Josh – Teratta spokesperson

Heillan (Hyle'-lan) – Agarian leader

In the Rocaran Domain

Tablar Ken – First Satran of the Rocaran Domain

Dahtra Selia (Dah'-trah Sell-lee-ah) – Current Satran

Aluta Seder (Ah-loo'-tah See'-der) – Dahtra's assistant

Rulian Trace (Roo'-lee-ahn) – Tarkan Region Administrator

Kemel Bosin – Rulian's assistant

Ilanni Tone (I-lahn'-ee) – Rocaran manager Planet Eltan

Herata Demis (Hair-ah'-tah) - Umbartran Administrator

Jerad Solbe – Terellan Region Administrator

Cartran Herc – Xartan (Zar-Tan) Region Administrator

Salus Donar – Cartran's assistant

Garan Ratra – Materan Region Administrator

Milan Chatrec – Military Administrator

Septcium – (Sept-see'-um) Rocaran leadership Council

Tezaxt – (Tez- axed') Rocaran Ritual Combat for Ascendency

Pax – Latin word for Peace

Planet Siana – Home Planet of the Rocaran

Tetara – Capital city of the Rocaran Domain on Siana

Planet Xarta – (Zar-ta) Xartan Region Headquarters
and home of the Xarta race

Planet Tarka – Tarkan Region Headquarters
and home of the Ortari race

Artis (Ar'-tiss) – Ortari village leader

Planet Eltan – In the Tarkan Region, Capital City Rotahra
and home of the Batani race

Amdar Lid – Batani manager of Rotahra

Hocan Duar – Batani resistance leader

Urritan

Urritan (Urr'-eh-tahn) – An extinct ancient race

Merillian – Urritan name for the planet Tarka

Perillian – Urritan name for the planet Agar

Nahnra – AI managing the Chamber on Merillian

Part One: The Forests of Agar

1. To Agar

Sunaj Research Center, Frazier, Washington State

"Agar!"

Janus had received several one-word messages like this. The first one had been a whispered *"yes"* in response to questions he had about himself and his role in the universe. The communications were softer than a telepathic thought. The "voice" itself seemed to emanate from an incalculably large but insubstantial Entity. As vast as Janus was, comprised of all consciousness on Earth, he felt small in comparison.

Janus concentrated on each brief message he received. He learned there was additional, unvoiced information. While concentrating, suddenly he became aware of something that he hadn't known before. This was the first message of this type, which requested Janus do something.

Attached to *"Agar"* was the feeling that Agar was a planet, that it was urgent that he "go" there and have Humans follow him. Agar's location was highlighted on a map of the galaxy. Janus was given knowledge to make sense of the "map," so he "knew" where he was to go, but there was no information about why. He didn't have any indication whether he would be leading the Humans into danger or not. Once Janus had absorbed the message, he contacted Sam Baxter.

Sam was with Carmen Willathorpe and Jesse Chavez in Sam's office at Sunaj, an H2 research facility. They were discussing the status of the projects on the Garduk planet Solan and the Sudahlli planet Thahll. Sam thought that those projects were far enough along that Carmen and Jesse could move on to something else if they wanted to. Carmen and Jesse weren't as sure as Sam was, until Janus began talking to them about the message he had received.

"That's an unusual new friend you have, Janus," Carmen said. "Do you think it is the planet Agar itself that is calling for help?"

"No, Carmen," Janus said. "I have the impression that the Entity that has been communicating with me is immense, floating freely in the vastness of space, and is not connected to a single planet. Until I have a better name for it, I have been thinking of it as the Entity. I have been receiving these messages for a few months. They have been providing me with interesting knowledge about the galaxy. I do not know the source or why it is passing along the knowledge."

"Maybe it has been giving you the information so you will be prepared to do something like what it is requesting in this message," said Jesse.

"That makes sense," Janus answered.

"That does seem likely," Sam said, "but we still don't know why it wants you to go to this planet and take us with you."

Carmen, ever the professional anthropologist said, "When I have gone into the field to study a tribe, I have learned that it is critical to avoid making assumptions about what I'll find or what anything means ahead of time. Maybe our friend wants us to see whatever the situation is ourselves."

"I understand your point, Carmen," Jesse said, "but we are completely in the dark with this one. In your example, at least you knew you were going to visit a tribe in a remote setting on Earth. We don't know what we will find on Agar. Something there might be lethal to us, and Janus's friend might not know that."

Carmen didn't say anything, but nodded, acknowledging the possibility.

"Based on the feeling, Janus, do you have an idea who should go with you?" asked Sam.

"As is often the case with these communications this message was vague on many points including the one you mention."

"When the Cheneshi asked us to go to Ocean to help them with their problem," Jesse said, "we had a pretty good idea what the problem was. That information allowed us to put together an appropriate team of scientists. In this case it doesn't sound like it's someone on the planet asking us to make the trip, but some unknown Entity who hasn't said why. I think that means in this case we should use a small team to make an initial assessment."

"It sounds interesting to me," Carmen said. "I'd like to be on the team. I get your point about the possible danger, Jesse. We'll have to proceed with caution, but the mystery is compelling."

"I didn't say I was scared off because of the unknowns," Jesse said. "Besides if you're going I'd like to be there with you."

Sam laughed, and said, "You two will need supervision, so I better go along."

They discussed other possible members and decided to limit it to just the three of them.

"Janus, you came to us, but there are eight billion Humans on Earth. Should we select any others for this first trip?"

"You have the most experience, Sam. I think the three of you are the right ones to assess the situation."

Of all the Lorengi ships, they were used to working with Thelika. They asked the Lorengi, Ahleeto, if they could use Thelika. She agreed and then asked to go with them.

They didn't know anything about the planet, so they prepared for jungles, mountains, forests and cities. As usual, the subject of weapons didn't come up. There might be danger as Jesse suggested, but their past experiences had shown them that they could protect themselves without weapons. They didn't like the message being armed would convey.

They let a few people at Sunaj know what they were doing. Sam also needed to contact his wife, U. S. Senator, Lesley Anderson. Not knowing exactly where she was or what she was doing, Sam thought telepathy would work best.

"So you don't know where you are going, only that it is thousands of light-years from here, and you don't know why you are going or what you'll find when you get there?" Lesley observed.

"That pretty much sums it up," Sam said.

"Except for the 'light-years' part of it, what you describe sounds like some of the meetings I get invited to."

Sam laughed. *"I'm hoping this will be more fun than the meetings you have told me about."*

"Me too. Let me know what you find and come back alive. After all these years, I've kind of gotten used to you."

"I will do my best on both counts."

* * *

Sam, Carmen and Jesse teleported themselves and their gear aboard the Lorengi ship. They met in Thelika's common room where they found Ahleeto. They discussed how to approach the mission and the planet. Thelika, like all the Lorengi ships was sentient and was able to instantly teleport across vast distances as long as there were coordinates available for the destination. The message Janus received included sufficient information for Thelika to locate Agar's star.

The trip to Agar took them seven thousand light-years away from Earth and closer to the Galactic Center. Before approaching Agar, they assessed the star system. The star was a little older than Earth's sun, but with similar spectral characteristics. Agar was the only habitable planet in the system from a Human perspective. It was approximately the same size as Earth, and roughly the same distance from its sun as Earth is from Sol. After this quick assessment, Thelika moved into a high-altitude orbit around the planet. Janus, of course, had traveled there on his own, and was waiting there when they arrived.

"It looks like the land surface is nearly covered with forest," Carmen observed, "but it's not a dense forest. The trees seem to have enough space between them to allow sunlight to reach the ground around them. There are a number of open areas. The trees are spread over all the land masses."

"There is no artificial light or radiation of any kind that I can detect, having made one trip around the planet," Thelika observed.

"What about life forms?" Ahleeto asked.

"I detect mobile thermal sources on land and in the oceans," Thelika observed. "Imagery is limited, due to the forests, and it is not possible to gain clear images beneath the water's surface."

"What about sentient beings?" Sam asked. "Janus, can you help us? Janus?"

The lack of response from Janus created an uneasy silence in Thelika's common room.

"Yes. Sorry for the delay, Sam. There is something very different here. I'm still trying to make sense of it. Setting that aside for the moment, I detect one sentient race of creatures in the oceans, and a different one moving about on land.

6

"It is difficult for me to provide an accurate physical description of either race, but the one on land is clearer to me. What I have comes from my looking through the eyes of one of them as they are looking at another. Since I have no context, I cannot determine their size.

"They have one head, two arms and two legs, all in the likely places. Their garments are simple. From what I can see of their bodies outside their garments, they are covered with short fur. They appear to live in shelters in the trees, and in villages, rather than cities. The population appears to be small and dispersed across the globe."

"Can you pick up anything about the race in the ocean, Janus?" Jesse asked.

"The images are much less distinct, but they are what you might call mer-people. They have long, slender bodies with a head at one end and a single fin at the other. They have two appendages near the head and two others midway down length of their body. These limbs appear to have webbed hand-like features at their ends. Their population is also small. They are in all parts of the oceans but are mostly concentrated near land masses."

It seemed natural, based on her experience, for Carmen to outline how to prepare for their landing.

"Thank you, Janus," Carmen said. "I'm sure we will need to call on your help throughout our visit. I say we visit one of the villages. We should carry small packs with water and rations for a couple of days. We will test the local food and water, but we shouldn't count on them being safe to consume."

"Thelika please pick a spot near one of the villages in a temperate zone of the planet," Ahleeto requested.

"I have located what looks to be a good landing area," Thelika said. "I should report that the planet's temperate zone extends across nearly all latitudes between the two poles. You will find the temperatures comfortable near where you will land. The nighttime temperatures are slightly cooler. The air is similar in content to the atmosphere on Earth."

"That helps us choose our clothing," Carmen said. "I advise that we dress comfortably in natural fabrics. The exception would be to include a hooded rain slicker in our packs. With that much vegetation, I imagine there will be a good deal of moisture."

"Should I come?" Ahleeto asked. "I would love to be with the landing party, but with the low-tech culture, my presence might frighten the villagers."

"I'll defer to Carmen," Sam said, "but I would suggest that you remain aboard Thelika until we can get a feeling for how the locals react."

Carmen turned to Ahleeto.

"I agree with Sam's take on it. Can you wait until we get to know the locals better?"

"Of course."

Thelika said, "Don't forget to take the small field recorders to pin to the front of your shirts. With those and your implants, Ahleeto and I will be able to track what you see and hear."

"Thanks for the reminder, Thelika," Carmen said. "That makes me feel a little better about leaving you behind, Ahleeto."

"We will be fine, Carmen," Ahleeto said. "We will be busy gathering data about the planet and keeping track of you at the same time."

Sam, Carmen and Jesse dressed carefully to appear non-threatening. They teleported to the location that Thelika had chosen, a small open space in the forest about three hundred yards from the village. The temperature and humidity on this bright sunny day were comfortable as Thelika had predicted. They looked at the surrounding forest and noticed that although one variety of trees was dominant in this area, there were other varieties striving for a place in the sunlight.

This was a different planet under a different sun, but the trees were various shades of green similar to what would be found on Earth. The dominate variety appeared to be comparable to coniferous varieties on Earth. Other trees were near the open area where they landed. These trees appeared to shed leaves, the evidence being on the ground around them. The conifer-like trees were enormous. The trunks were near twenty feet across, with branches nearly half that thick at the lower levels. The trees soared toward the sky attaining heights of more than two hundred feet.

The trees were fascinating, but they could investigate them in more detail later. They adjusted their packs and walked in the direction of the nearby village. When they came to the village edge they were able to see the villagers walking around and doing tasks. The villagers were as Janus described. The Humans could now add one crucial feature to the description. The local adults were between four and five feet tall. The villagers had two eyes separated by a small, fur-less, black nose. Their ears were flat to the sides of their heads. Their mouths were proportional to the size of their head.

There were two children running around in the village. When they saw the strangers, they ran around them, making sounds that sounded like laughter, and then ran off again. The adults that noticed their arrival raised their head and smiled. No one in the village seemed frightened.

One adult rose and came over to them, smiling. Carmen couldn't be sure, but she thought it was a female. The villager spread her arms out with palms open. She motioned for them to come into the village and led them to the center, where a tree-like material in the middle of the village had grown bent over into the shape of a bench large enough for several people to sit on.

She gestured for them to sit on the bench. When they did another adult brought something like hollowed out gourds and a container that appeared to have been carved into the shape of a pitcher from dark wood. That person poured what looked like water into the gourds and handed one to each of the visitors. Both adults used hand motions encouraging them to drink the liquid.

Carmen smiled at their hosts, raised the gourd to her mouth. She was concerned about the safety of drinking an unknown liquid. At the same time she didn't want to offend their hosts.

"Thelika," Carmen whispered through her implant, "can you remotely analyze the water in this gourd?"

"All I can tell you is that there are no live microorganisms in the water," Thelika answered. "I cannot do a conclusive chemical analysis."

"Thanks."

That provided some assurance for Carmen. She also felt that the villagers knew the liquid would not harm them. She smelled the contents. When she found no offensive odor, she sipped from the gourd. It tasted like the water it appeared to be. She couldn't detect anything harmful. So she took another sip.

Carmen looked at their hosts and said, "Thank you."

Their hosts, nodded, smiled and walked away, leaving the visitors in stunned silence. They had come as strangers into a primitive village. Not only were the villagers unperturbed, they seemed to understand the presence of the visitors, almost as if the villagers were expecting them.

2. A Village of Trees

Planet Agar

Carmen turned to her companions and raised her gourd.

"I think this water is safe to drink."

Sam and Jesse both took a sip and then drank the water in their gourds. They looked around the village.

"They are taking our presence calmly enough," Jesse said.

Carmen noticed it, too. "That is odd. It seems unlikely that they get visitors every day. Also, I could swear the one that gave us the water understood me when I said, 'Thank you.' Something unusual is going on here."

"Speaking of unusual, look at these trees," Sam said. The trees formed a circle around the central courtyard in which they were sitting. "They have formed themselves to make shelters for these people. The openings in the trunks weren't carved from the tree. See how the bark is continuous around the frame of the doorway. The smaller branches on the side look like steps to the upper levels."

Jesse pointed to the upper levels. "There are more openings in the trunk up there. It's like a multi-story home."

"The large branches provide natural pathways between the trees above the ground," Carmen said. "The branches must be six or seven feet in diameter."

"This bench we are sitting on is also a natural growth," Sam said. "This is very interesting."

"Perhaps when we learn to communicate with them we'll learn more," Carmen said.

The villager who had led them to the bench ran over to them and gestured for them to follow her. She led them to one of the shelters, and urged them to go in. Carmen noticed that all of the villagers were seeking shelter. The Humans ducked down to get through the shorter door, stepped over the four-inch-high wooden threshold, and entered the shelter.

The outside light dimmed as dark clouds rapidly blocked out the sunlight. In the next instant, a drenching downpour began. The torrential rain fell for ten minutes flooding the village area that they had just been sitting in.

The rain stopped as quickly as it had begun. The clouds dispersed. Sunlight reflected off the water in the courtyard and other wet surfaces. A few minutes later, the water sank below the spongy, peat-like vegetation that covered the courtyard. The villagers went outside and resumed their activities as if such showers were a routine occurrence. Sam and the others following the villager's lead went out and resumed their previous activity—sitting on the bench.

"Curiouser and Curiouser," Jesse said.

"Yes, but at least we haven't been asked to go down a rabbit hole," Carmen added. "I'm probably just stating the obvious, but the phenomena we have witnessed in the last few minutes are astounding. These people appear to be in a close symbiosis with their environment."

"Perhaps that extends to their fearless welcome when we arrived," Sam suggested.

"What do you mean?" Jesse asked.

"Maybe there has never been anything in their experience besides them and their environment," Sam said. "Could our welcome come from an assumption on their part that we are a natural development too—something new, but still part of the whole?"

"Or perhaps their environment informed them of your arrival, and that you might need a drink of water," Janus offered.

"Is that an informed opinion, Janus, or are you guessing like we are?" Jesse asked.

"More than a guess, but not quite an informed opinion. When we arrived I said that something was different here. I've had time to investigate my vague feeling."

"Any conclusions?" Sam asked.

"This planet is alive!"

"I assume you mean more than there is organic life here," Jesse said.

"Yes. I don't fully understand what I have found, or its implications, but Agar is giving off emanations of a large, organic being."

"You mean it is the amalgamation of all consciousness on the planet like you are on Earth?" Carmen asked.

"No. I mean it appears to me to be a planet-sized organic being. Yes, it has a planet-sized consciousness, but it is made up of organic material, not just consciousness. It's like one of you, only larger."

"Do you think Agar is the being that asked you to come here?" Sam asked.

"No, Agar is not the Entity that has been sending me these enigmatic communications."

"So, we're here," Carmen said, summing up. "Agar is interesting, and it seems safe here. There are many things to learn about it. Should we conclude that at least part of the reason we were asked to come here is to learn about this unusual planet?"

"That may not be all of it, Carmen, but my feeling is that it is an important part of the reason my puzzling friend asked us to travel to Agar. I think we are to learn all we can about this unique being."

13

"Was learning that Agar was one, large, sentient being what caused you to think that it may have given the information about our arrival to these villagers?" Jesse asked.

"Yes, though the nature of that communication is unknown. I assume that Agar decided that we mean no harm and suggested that the welcome you received was the appropriate response. I do not know the history of this planet. We might be the first visitors. It might not know what to make of us. We might be on a sort of probationary status, being watched and judged."

"Have you tried to communicate with Agar?"

"Yes, I have Sam. I do not feel competent to make this assessment, but I think that sentience is relatively new to Agar's consciousness. It has a limited ability to communicate. It seemed apprehensive when we first arrived. I believe I was able to convey that we were here to learn about the planet, not to harm it in any way."

"Well, I certainly don't want to make a planet mad at us," Jesse said.

"I agree," Carmen said. "I don't think we will if we proceed carefully. Janus, it will help if you keep a connection with our host. You could let us know how we are doing in Agar's opinion."

"Yes. I'll keep you posted."

"Thanks. I was wondering about something that happened. It seemed to me that one of the locals understood my words when I spoke to them. Is it possible that Agar somehow learned our language, maybe through you, and transferred that knowledge to these people? The Cheneshi learned our language through you."

"The situation with the Cheneshi was different, Carmen. When we contacted the Cheneshi, there was a purposeful exchange of massive amounts of data. I learned about them, and they learned about us. The Cheneshi are very intelligent

and articulate. We don't know the capability of Agar or its people."

"I guess it is different here, but I thought I saw a glimmer of understanding. Thanks, Janus."

"You're welcome, Carmen. I will let you all know of any developments in my work with Agar."

Carmen turned to Sam and Jesse who were next to her on the bench.

"We need to start interacting with our hosts to learn more. Have you noticed that the adults haven't said a word to each other?" Carmen asked.

"Yes," Jesse said, "but they seem to be communicating. They use gestures, but to me, those gestures don't communicate much."

"Could they be telepathic?" Sam asked.

"Let's try verbal communication first," Carmen said.

To the Humans, the villagers all looked very much the same. They wore simple pants and tunics. There was a rope-like belt drawing the tunic together at the waist. Some were taller than others. It was not obvious which were male or female, if genders were part of their physiology.

Carmen thought she knew who had welcomed and guided them out of the rain. She walked over to where the villager was weaving a basket and sat down on her knees.

"Thank you for the water and helping us get out of the rain."

The local looked up into Carmen's eyes, smiled and nodded, and then went back to weaving. Carmen couldn't determine if she had been understood, or if the villager was just politely nodding even though they didn't understand. She tried a more direct approach.

"Do you understand the words I am using?"

The weaver looked up again and nodded. Carmen was beginning to doubt her basic communication skills as an

15

anthropologist when another villager came out of a nearby shelter. This one was taller than the villager who gave her the water, and perhaps more muscular. Carmen thought that this one might be male. As she was working on that thought the new villager spoke.

"She does understand you, but like the rest of us, she is very uneasy with the new information and language we've been given."

3. A Part of Agar

Carmen looked up at the new villager, and turned her head toward Sam and Jesse, who had already risen to be ready in case the new arrival meant to harm Carmen. Sam and Jesse both shrugged in the timeless, Human way. They gestured with their hands for her to go ahead, as if saying, "You're the anthropologist."

She rolled her eyes, gave them a thanks-a-lot look, and rose to her feet. She turned to the new arrival and bowed slightly.

"As you can imagine, we are surprised that you can speak our language," Carmen said.

"As we would be if you were able to speak ours. I am called Johar."

His voice had a bass tone, which reinforced Carmen's Human-based impression that Johar and the other taller villagers might be male. He was relaxed. More relaxed than Carmen would have been had three of Agar's people arrived in her backyard.

"I am called Carmen. My friends are Sam and Jesse," she said, pointing to each as she spoke their names.

Johar bowed.

"Welcome, Carmen. Welcome Sam and Jesse," Johar said.

"How did our language come to you?" Carmen asked.

"As all things come to us, from the world we live on. Before this new information came to us, we did not have a name for our world. We just thought of ourselves as 'the people,' and all things were provided by our world. Now that our world has adopted the name Agar, we will call ourselves, Agara, the people of Agar."

These people were used to thinking of the world that now calls itself Agar as the provider. Carmen wondered if the 'Agara' knew that their 'world' was a planet floating in space. That seemed unlikely given their apparent lack of technology to see the stars.

"Where did the language that came to Agar come from?"

"From outside. It was meant for us, and Agar passed it to us."

"Do you know how the language came to Agar?"

"Agar doesn't know. One moment it was not there, the next it was."

Carmen paused for a moment to communicate with Janus and her two colleagues.

"Does that sound familiar, Janus?"

"Yes, it does remind me of the way I have been acquiring knowledge from my new friend. I think it is likely that Agar received its information from the same source and received it in support of the mission that brought us here."

"You seem very calm for one who is learning things that are very different from your past experience, Johar," Carmen said.

"We are calm, because Agar is in accord with these new developments."

"You are using our language very well."

"We are aware of more than our simple way of life. What Agar knows, all parts of Agar know, each to its ability to understand. We know that Agar is a planet that revolves around our sun. We know of the life on the planet. We know our part in that life."

"Forgive me if I have offended you, or Agar," Carmen said. "There are many things we are obviously unaware of. Perhaps if we could spend time with you, we would learn."

"Agar is not offended, nor am I. It is our understanding that the reason for your visit is to learn about Agar. We will gladly tell you about us and our world. In the process, perhaps you could share your knowledge with us and thus Agar."

The conversation with Johar apparently encouraged the others in the village. Those not already in the courtyard came out to greet the visitors.

Carmen looked at the group. A number, like Johar, were taller. If his type was male, it appeared there were about an equal number of males and females in the village. All together there were about forty villagers. There seemed to be only the two children that they saw when first entering the village. Carmen looked at Sam and Jesse.

"I wonder if this is the entire village. If so, there appears to be about the same number of males and females, but I would expect that there would be more children."

"Let's ask if there are more somewhere else," Jesse suggested.

"I agree that would be the most direct route, but let's talk of other things to see what we can find out."

Carmen looked at the person who had welcomed them into the village and asked, "What is your name?"

"I am Sela," she said.

"Thank you for welcoming us to your village."

Sela smiled and nodded.

Carmen turned to the one who had brought them the water. "What is your name?"

"I am Tana."

"Thank you for giving us water, Tana."

"You are welcome," Tana said. "Agar thought you would be thirsty, and that it was safe for you to drink our water."

"Where do you come from?" one of the children asked. The child's voice and demeanor seemed like an adult.

Carmen couldn't be sure but now that she looked at the children, they both seemed to have the slighter builds and the features of those she thought of as females.

"What's your name?" Sam asked.

"Sarra," she answered.

"Well, Sarra," Sam said, "we come from a planet far away. Do you know what a planet is?"

"Of course, Agar is a planet. How can you be away from your planet?"

Sam looked to Jesse and Carmen.

Jesse jumped in, "Our minds are still connected to our planet."

"Oh," Sarra said. She nodded. It didn't look like she understood Jesse's answer. It was more like she had to think about it before she would ask other questions.

From the wide-eyed looks of the adults in the village and the murmurs in the group, it seemed that others were having trouble comprehending being away from one's planet or what connecting by mind alone would be like.

Carmen saw their reaction. It confirmed something she was beginning to feel about these people. She conveyed her theory to Sam and Jesse.

"These people aren't on Agar with a life separate from their planet. The Agara are part of Agar. They are their planet. Our interpretation of Johar's statement that the Agara were the people of Agar was that they were the people on the planet Agar, like Humans, or whales on Earth. I don't think that's the situation here. In this case it means that the Agara are the people-part of Agar, similar to the tree-part, or the water-part. All of what we see around is part of the larger organic being that is Agar."

Her companions looked at her, letting the distinction sink in and nodding as it did.

As if sensing the awkwardness of the moment, Johar said, "It is different for our visitors than it is for us. We will learn from each other. As we learn from these visitors Agar and all Agara will learn."

"Telepaths?" Jesse asked.

"Maybe," Janus answered, *"but to me it sounds more like how the information about us was transferred in advance of our arrival. When Agar learned of it all the information was given to the Agara."*

"Let us take time to allow what we have already learned settle into our awareness," Johar said. "Perhaps our visitors would like to rest, or walk through the forest to learn more about Agar?"

"That would be good, Johar," Carman said. "Could you show us where we could shelter while we are visiting your village?"

Johar turned to Sela and asked, "Would you mind interrupting your basket weaving to show our visitors to their shelter?"

Sela nodded. Carmen had to wonder if that was Johar delegating or Agar deciding that it was the best way to get the job done.

Sam asked Johar, "May we wander through the forest after we get settled?"

"Of course, Sam. You may encounter creatures in the forest. They might come up to you to look at you and catch your scent. No part of Agar will harm you, so you needn't fear these creatures."

Sela led Carmen, Sam and Jesse to the side of one of the large trees and climbed up what Sam had identified as the smaller branches that were used as steps. They followed her up one level. She turned and started out across one of the large branches that served as pathways between trees. Even though the seven-foot diameter branch would have been wide enough to walk across if it were rounded on top. The Humans were glad that the top surface was flat.

Sela stopped at the entrance of a shelter in a neighboring tree and gestured for them to enter. With this shelter they didn't have to bend over to get through the door, and they found it was tall enough on the inside for them to stand. The room was circular, about fifteen feet in diameter. The walls were covered with a bark that was smoother than the bark on the outside of the tree. There were three window-like openings which let light into the small room.

There were three flat surfaces which looked like they were meant for sleeping. They were long enough for the Humans to sleep on, and the platforms could be used to sit on as well. There was a basin protruding from the wall, and a continuous stream of water flowing into it from a spigot jutting out of the tree wall above it. The water drained back into the tree. There was no table surface, so apparently this was not an eating room.

"Is this room set aside for visitors?" Sam asked.

Sela looked at him in disbelief.

"You are the first visitors to Agar. This room was made when Agar learned you would be coming."

Astonished, Sam said, "You mean that this section of the tree was solid just days before?"

"Of course. What else would it be?"

"How was the room made?"

"Agar had the tree adjust itself."

While Sam and Jesse were looking around the room, trying to fathom how a mature tree could be reshaped Carmen asked about visitors again.

"Have there been visitors to other villages?"

"No. You are the first visitors to Agar. Wait!"

Sela held up her hand and paused as if listening to someone.

"You are the first visitors to be on Agar, but another sky vessel came, and circled the planet. Agar didn't like the feel of them, and he let them know they were not welcome."

"Janus, how would Agar let someone know they weren't welcome?" Carmen asked.

"Agar does not seem articulate, so I don't think it was with words. I believe it would have been by sending a strong feeling. I haven't felt the full power of Agar's emotions, but the little I have felt lead me to believe that if it became upset, anyone near would get a very strong feeling indeed."

"Lucky we are on the invitee list," Carmen said.

"Yes."

"Thank you Sela. Your forests are very thick with these magnificent trees. I hope we don't get lost," Carmen said, just to make conversation. They could always teleport back to their room now that they knew its location.

Sela took Carmen's expressed concern seriously. "Do not worry. Agar knows where you are at all times. Agar knew when you arrived in your sky vessel. He knew when you left it to be on the planet, though I sense that he is unsure how you did that. When you are walking in the forest you will receive guidance. When you wish to return to our village again, you will know the rightness or wrongness of your steps."

"Will Agar give us a feeling in the same way that he gave those in the sky vessel a feeling that he they were not welcome?"

"No. It is different for you. You have breathed Agar's air. You have drunk Agar's water. You will know the right way, because a part of Agar is in you."

4. The Joshua Tree

Sela left the visitors. They mumbled their goodbyes, thinking about the unknown implications of the last thing she said.

"Be careful what you drink," Jesse said smiling. "I didn't see that coming. We cannot hold our breath the entire time we are here. I suppose we will continue to accumulate parts of our host as we go."

"Yes," Carmen said. "We can't avoid it, so let's just wait and see the ramifications of carrying part of Agar with us. I'm glad we planned ahead, and left blood samples and other biometrics for each of us with Thelika before we came to the surface. Ahleeto can use the ships lab to compare those with the results when we want to leave the surface again. The Lorengi had to be careful when they visited new planets. We will take the same precautions.

"It does raise a general issue for us. Since coming here, we have encountered unusual things. A tree on Agar can reshape itself, and we have part of Agar in us now. My point is these things are natural to the Agara. Let us absorb these new facts calmly without making a big deal of them. We are here to learn about Agar and the Agara. We can be amazed certainly, but let's not show it. I think the information transfer will flow better if we note the differences and move on."

"In that spirit, let's go for a walk in the forest," Sam said, "and give our new planet-sized guidance system a test."

It's what they intended to do anyway, so learning that Agar would be with them didn't change their plans. They kept their packs on, thus leaving nothing in their assigned room, and walked back the way they came and down to the village floor. As they walked through the courtyard and out of the village, the villagers they encountered smiled and then returned to what they were doing. Carmen thought that her advice to her colleagues to take things in stride seemed to be the way the Agara were reacting to the presence of the Humans.

They left the village on the opposite side from where they entered it earlier. The forest floor contained more of the peat-like vegetation under the trees, like what was on the ground in the village. Where the sunlight touched the ground grass-like vegetation sprouted. As soon as they left the habitat of the Agara, they were surrounded by the enormous trees. Soon they felt they were walking in a forest similar to those on Earth.

There were sounds of creatures in the forest, and the buzz of some flying insect they couldn't see. There was a gentle breeze stirring the branches above them. The branches of the trees began about seven feet above the ground. There were none of the small step-branches of the trees in the village. Apparently they grew when there was a need for them. They gained proof that this was true when they were about a hundred yards into the forest.

"It would be great to climb one of these fabulous trees," Jesse said. "Imagine the view you would have."

Jesse had his hands on one of the trees. He was leaning towards it and looking up to its top. There was a rumbling sound from inside the tree followed by small step-branches emerging from the side of the tree he was touching. They led to the first major branch. Additional step-branches emerged above which would facilitate the climb. They couldn't see how far up the step-branches went, but if they were responding to Jesse's wish, they would allow him to get to the top.

The three Humans shared another moment of stunned silence that had become common since their arrival on Agar.

Recovering, Sam said, "On this world 'be careful what you wish for' apparently is good advice. There is probably a scientific explanation for this, but it looks like magic to me. Well, tree-climber, you asked for an opportunity to see the view. Looks like you have been given one."

"I did," Jesse said. "Anyone want to join me?"

Sam said he would. Carmen opted to stay on the ground to study the forest from that level. She watched them climb as long as she could see them through the thick branches. She took the opportunity of being alone to study her surroundings.

She sat on the forest floor with her back to the tree her companions were climbing. She closed her eyes and sought to see the workings of the forest with her mind-view. Immediately she was aware of the internal activity of the tree she was leaning against and that of all the vegetation around her.

The tree was more active, more fluid than those on Earth or the planet Ocean where she had used her mind to study them in a similar fashion. Carmen could now understand how the tree could extend these step-branches when needed or hollow out a room for visitors. Its ability to morph into various shapes gave her the feeling that the tree might be alive in the sense of having some level of sentience. After all, unless Agar itself made the tree change, this tree responded to Jesse's thought. A tree having sentience wasn't so strange an idea. The members of the sentient race on Ocean, the Cheneshi, were trees.

She attempted to communicate with the tree telepathically.

"Hello. Can you understand me?"

"Yes, though it is strange to communicate so. We 'trees,' as you call us, only are able to communicate with each other. The people of the village feel Agar, but do not communicate with us as you do. It is understandable, because they are young, but so are you. How is it you can do this?"

26

Amazing, Carmen thought to herself. If it knew they called them 'trees' she wondered if they could understand their thoughts when they spoke out loud.

"Can you understand my thoughts when I vocalize them?"

"Yes, but it is clearer in this mode."

"Okay. Are you Agar?"

"Yes and no. We are of Agar, but Agar is the whole. We are only part of Agar. We are the oldest part."

This was exciting, Carmen thought. Could these trees tell her the history of this unusual planet? Not wanting to go too fast, she changed the subject.

"Thank you for providing the steps for my friends to climb. Will they be safe?"

"I will keep them safe. Please answer my question!"

Its question? What question? Then she remembered.

"There are among my people those who can communicate with their minds. We call it telepathy. Sam and Jesse who are climbing you now are able to do that. It just hasn't occurred to them to communicate with you. I am able to do so, because a member of another race of 'trees' on another planet had to alter my mind to save my life."

"Extraordinary. Do you mind if my neighbors listen in. They are as fascinated as I am with this conversation."

"That would be fine. To us you look like trees of our world. So far as we are aware, our trees cannot communicate like this. Do you have a name you call yourselves, or will 'trees' be sufficient?"

"Sometime in the past, we chose to call ourselves a name to differentiate us from the rest of Agar. That name is Teratta. We have not had occasion to use it much because we only communicate among ourselves. You can use Teratta when speaking about us. If you call us 'trees' that will be acceptable also.

"My kind are called Human. My individual name is Carmen. Do you have an individual name?"

"No."

"For convenience of conversation, do you mind if I give you a name?

"What do you have in mind?"

"I would call you Josh, short for Joshua tree, which is among the oldest trees on our planet."

"'Josh,' I like that."

"Good. Josh, we are here to learn about your planet and those who live upon it. You said you 'trees' are the oldest part of Agar. Could you explain?"

"I will if you will tell me more about your kind and those 'trees' you speak of that live on another planet."

Carmen imagined what it would be like for the Teratta to be connected to Sways and the other Cheneshi, or Janus for that matter. It might be too great a shock for these isolated trees. It would be better to give them some background to help with the transition. It would also be good to know what they are already aware of in their isolated state.

"I will. There is much for both of us to tell but let us begin slowly. You say you are the oldest part of Agar. What does that mean?"

"Agar is an old planet, Carmen. It began sprouting life a very long time ago, in the oceans and on the land where we live. We were the first large beings created."

"You mean the earlier versions of you, the first Teratta?"

"I think you must have misunderstood me. I mean us. Those Teratta you see around you are the 'first' Teratta."

"How long ago were you created?"

"Since the first few of us were created Agar has gone around its star a multitude of times."

If Carmen compared what the tree was saying with Earth's planetary history, the earliest large plants like this tree would have formed hundreds of millions of years ago. Was this tree saying that it and its neighbors are that old? She must have misunderstood. On Earth the oldest trees are a thousand years old, some are a few hundred years. Most are less than a hundred years old.

"I hope you don't mind, Carmen, but I was listening to your thoughts as you pondered what I said. Your planet's history is different from my vague understanding of Agar's. The oldest Teratta have lived on Agar millions of years not hundreds of millions. Of course we didn't all come at once. There was a process of propagation which continued until we filled the land. No additional Teratta were needed, so the propagation stopped. Nor were we able to communicate as we are now. That began much later in our history."

"That is surprising. On our planet, the process of life includes decay and death, which limit the length of time an organic life form can stay in its form."

A shudder ran through the tree. Carmen heard Sam and Jesse shout from above.

"Josh, my friends!"

"I have kept them safe," Josh said. After a pause he continued. *"Your explanation of life on your planet was so terrible I couldn't keep myself from shaking in response to the thought."*

"Isn't that the way of things on Agar?"

"There is decay if I understand your meaning of that word. Parts of me stop functioning properly, but they are repaired, and I go on."

Regeneration! Across eons! Josh explained it simply enough, but it was amazing.

"Is it the same for the people of the village?" Carmen asked, not sure she wanted the answer.

"No."

Whew! Carmen thought, but then Josh continued.

"The people of the village are much younger. To use your time scale, they began as part of Agar only about one hundred thousand years ago."

"Are all parts of Agar sustained in this manner?"

"Yes, for those you would call sentients. There is constant change, constant movement. Matter is exchanged from one life-form to another, sustaining both through some internal process. I am not certain about the people in the Oceans, but I think it likely that they are sustained in the same way. I cannot imagine the process you described that exists on your planet."

"I understand your problem," Carmen said, ironically.

Just then, Carmen heard noise from above. Sam and Jesse were descending. Carmen was interested what their reaction would be when she told them that the tree they had just climbed was alive and sentient.

"How was the view?" Carmen asked, when they were both on the ground.

"Fantastic," Jesse said. "The dark green of the branches of these trees extends in all directions with only a few breaks, like the open space we landed in."

"I agree with Jesse," Sam said. "The other thing I noticed was that there were no mountains. I wonder if the volcanism that is often associated with planet formation was less active here."

"Why don't you ask Josh?" Carmen said, and then laughed at the looks on their faces.

She let them wonder what she meant for a moment, and then told them about the Teratta. They both looked at the tree they had just climbed with a new regard.

Jesse nonchalantly patted the side of the tree and said, "Thanks for the climbing steps, Josh."

"You are welcome, Jesse."

"He knows my name?"

"Yes, I told Josh the names of the people climbing on him."

"And he can pick up our thoughts when we speak?" Sam asked.

"Yes, though Josh says that it is better when we use telepathy."

"This is great," Jesse said. "Just like on Ocean, only we don't have to get wet, and we can climb them. If that's alright, I mean."

"Josh, is it alright to climb on you like we did?" Jesse asked.

"Yes. I enjoyed it. My neighbors would like you to climb on them, should you decide to climb again."

"Thanks."

"How does he know our language so well?" Sam asked. "Did he get the same download the Agara did?"

"Download?" Josh asked. *"What an interesting and descriptive term. If you are referring to the massive amount of knowledge about your kind that Agar received ahead of your arrival, then yes, I 'got the download.'"*

Carmen turned to her friends, smiling.

"There's more."

5. Quarantine?

"That's not possible," Sam said, after Carmen told them that the Teratta had been regenerated for eons.

"It certainly doesn't match what we think is possible," Carmen said, "but Josh was very clear."

"If it is true, this is a very unusual biosphere," Sam said. "How could it have happened here?"

Jesse assumed it was true when Carmen told him and was pondering the question that Sam had raised.

"Could this be an experiment?" Jesse asked. "Remember what the Annli Theron said about the unique aspects of our DNA being put in place on purpose? His notion was that the universe needed something like us, so it played with our DNA to see if the end result was close to what it was looking for. Maybe the universe was trying out something different here."

"...and we were asked to come and take a look?" Sam queried.

"Pretty far-fetched, huh?" Jesse offered.

"Theron's view of how our DNA was changed was also far-fetched, Jesse," Sam said. "We may never know the answer to that, or what started this biosphere on its unusual path. I guess one is as plausible as the other."

"Just as plausible and just as incomprehensible," Carmen said. "As you said, Sam, we may not know the answer to how either got started. I think we should ask ourselves what we are going to do with the latest hard-to-believe wonder we've been presented with."

"We check it out," Sam said.

"Do you mean try to see if it is true?" Jesse asked.

"That might be possible, Jesse, but I was thinking that we should see if the entire biosphere is involved. Let's go talk with the Agara and see what they think."

Carmen shot Sam a look.

"I know, Carmen, we will need to be careful how we go about it. That's why I suggest that you ask the questions."

Carmen looked at him for a moment longer, then relaxed and nodded. They made their way back to the village and were greeted with the same smiling acceptance that had been present from the beginning. Carmen walked over to Sela, sat on the ground near her, and watched as she finished the basket she was weaving.

The basket was made of fiber that had been woven into a rope about a half inch in diameter. The rope was then drawn in a circle held together by other thin fibers woven around each layer of rope as it made the bottom of the basket, and then was brought up to make the sides. The fibers were of varying shades of purple and gray, making a colorful basket.

Carmen watched Sela and thought about the fibers. That caused her to look at Sela's tunic and pants. They also seemed to be made of fiber. She asked Sela about it.

"It is the same fiber," Sela said. She pointed to the peat-like material covering the ground. "When we want to make a tunic or other garment we mash the fiber and soak it in water. It becomes sticky and can be made into the fabric our garments are made from."

Carmen nodded. It sounded something like making paper.

"Sela, I noticed that there are only two children in the village. Why are there only two?"

Sela's eyes became wide, and a smile crossed her face.

"They are such a joy and so rare. We are lucky to have them."

Carmen wasn't sure how to respond. Instead of answering her question, Sela had added new questions to the list. Carmen kept going.

"How do you mean 'rare'?" she asked.

"These are the only children on Agar. We are blessed that they are living with us. Agara from nearby villages often come by just to watch them play. All Agara are aware of the children but being aware is not the same as seeing them having fun running around."

Carmen looked at Sam and Jesse to see if they were making sense out of what Sela was saying. How could there be only two children on the entire planet? Her companions looked as dumbfounded as she was.

"I agree you are lucky to have the children in your village. Which of you is their mother?"

Sela looked at Carmen clearly not understanding the question. Carmen asked a different question.

"How did they come to be in your village?"

"Agar made them and sent them here."

"I apologize if I am asking a naive question, Sela, but how did Agar make them?"

"We don't know. One day, we heard unfamiliar chatter just outside the village. A short time later, these two children came in. Of course they were smaller then. We made garments for them, and we had two new little shes."

Carmen looked at Sam and Jesse again, who were struggling to keep their best taking-it-in-stride look on their faces.

"Do you know why Agar blessed you and this village with the children?"

Sela looked down as if not wanting to talk about something. She answered in a low voice. "We think it was because two shes from our village ended when they fell into a chasm not far from here. That, too, is something that has never happened before."

"I don't want to cause you discomfort with this question, but don't the Agara, end?"

Sela did her best to hide her shock but failed.

"What? Of course not. We have always been, since the beginning. Those were the first two who ended in our memory."

"I'm sorry, Sela. I didn't mean to upset you. Agara are special. It is that specialness that we are trying to understand."

Sela smiled, patted Carmen's arm with one of her hands, and nodded.

Carmen turned to Sam and Jesse.

"I think we have our verification. Regeneration is true for the Agara, as well."

The Humans sat in silence for a while, noting the activity in the village. If the other villagers had been eavesdropping during their conversation with Sela, it wasn't evident. They continued doing what they had been doing unperturbed. Johar had walked by once, nodding his greeting.

Some of the shes were weaving baskets, others looked like they might be preparing food. The visitors couldn't be sure since they had no concept what Agara food might look like. They had been on Agar too short a time to see usual feeding times. Food might not even be necessary with regeneration.

They stood and made their way to the room that had been set aside for them. When they arrived, they looked around the space with a new understanding. Carmen felt compelled to communicate with their home tree.

"Hello. Thank you for making room for us. I hope it isn't to inconvenient or uncomfortable for you."

"Quite the opposite, Carmen," the tree answered. *"I have the honor of providing a shelter for the only visitors that Agar*

has ever had. I have attained a good deal of notoriety as a result. All Teratta on Agar know of my honor."

"My friends and I will be here for a bit to discuss some of the wonders we have found on your beautiful planet. You're welcome to listen in. You can comment if you want to."

"Thank you, I will."

"Maybe the regeneration present in this biosphere is what we have been drawn here to observe," Carmen said.

"If that is so, does our observation have a purpose?" Sam asked. "What are we to do with his information?"

"Let's ask ourselves, what are the implications of our new knowledge?" Carmen said.

"The Agara, the Teratta and who knows what else live an enormously long time," Jesse said. "You might say they are immortal."

"Immortality!" Sam exclaimed. "Could that be it? Here it is natural. In the rest of the universe that we are aware of it is highly unnatural. It is also highly sought after. At least it has been on Earth. I think it likely is also sought by other races in our galaxy."

"Highly sought after," Carmen said, "and highly dangerous to most societies. Think of what it would do to the population on Earth. We think H2s will live long, but they have shorter fertility periods, and prefer fewer children. It would be a problem even with H2s, but H1s still make up eighty percent of the population. Widespread immortality among the population would doom our already overpopulated planet. I would think it would do the same for any race on any planet."

"Didn't Sela say that Agar had recent experience with the spaceship of another race?" Jesse asked. "It arrived and was encouraged to leave. We've been told that we are the first visitors to Agar. That may be true, but it looks like at least one other race has found the planet. Maybe we need to help with that somehow. Help keep others away from the planet."

"I agree," Sam said. "Once found this planet might look like it is possibly rich with resources to be exploited by a race bent on expansion and that is resource hungry. Is Agar vulnerable, though?"

"Whether it could defend itself, isn't the important question," Carmen observed. "If members of another race were to land, and leave again, they might never come back, but when leaving they might inadvertently be taking immortality with them—in their blood, on their clothes. If they discovered what we have found, they might find a way to take it away on purpose. Either scenario would spell disaster."

The three of them looked at each other, each recognizing the dire implication of Carmen's statement at the same time. They were part of a foreign race that had landed on Agar. When they departed....

"We have 'a part of Agar' in us," Jesse said. "What does that mean?"

"We don't know yet," Sam said. "Does it mean we have the seeds of regeneration in our bodies? If we left we would be that race you spoke of, Carmen."

"Do we have to spend the rest of what will be a very long life on Agar?" Carmen asked. "Were we called to Agar to be quarantined on this planet forever?"

6. Divided Attention

"We don't know what we have yet," Sam said. "So I think it's a bit early to begin decorating our tree house here for a long stay. Whatever has brought us here it probably wasn't just to trap three Humans on a remote planet. Something else is going on, and I have a feeling that we need to quickly find out what it is.

"We have to learn about the regeneration process. We also need to keep exploring Agar and find out if Agar has any more surprises for us. I believe we are here to gain a thorough understanding of this unusual planet, so we are prepared when the real reason we were brought here is revealed.

"It's been a while, but in the early years of Compass, I did a good deal of research to advance medical science. I will set up equipment here and on Thelika to discover what we need to know about regeneration on Agar and whether our bodies now contain what it takes to regenerate.

"I would like you two to continue to exploring Agar. We have one more sentient race to encounter—the one in the ocean. I think it would be wise to learn more about Agar through them."

Carmen and Jesse nodded.

"Is there anything you need from us to do the research, Boss?" Jesse asked, smiling.

Sam blinked and focused on his two stunned companions.

"I guess I got carried away. What do you two think?" Sam asked.

"Your plan sounds like a good one," Carmen said. "What you suggest is likely the quickest way to get the needed information."

"Okay," Sam said. "I'll start preparing for the research."

Sam sat down on one of the three platforms and began making notes on his comm pad. Carmen and Jesse looked at each other and left the shelter. Standing on the wide branch outside the door of the shelter they began to discuss what they would do next.

"Wow! I have never seen Sam so serious and determined," Jesse said.

Carmen agreed. "He's usually so relaxed, letting others make the decisions. It's a surprise to see this side of him, but in this circumstance I am glad Sam-the-leader has arrived on the scene."

"Me too. If his intuition is telling him that this is serious, then I'm willing to bet that it is. It's a bit scary, but it also motivates me to get going on our part. What do you suggest?"

"Well, two things. We need to connect with the 'mer-people' as Janus described them. Also, we have only seen a small part of the land surface of this planet. I think it would be a mistake to think that we know the planet from this small sample. Of the two, I think we should go to the ocean first."

"Sounds good. Let's go back aboard Thelika and get equipped to do some swimming. Do you think we should let our hosts know we are leaving?"

"Agar will probably let them know somehow, but I think we should."

They went to the village courtyard and told Sela that they would be leaving.

"Where will you go?" Sela asked. "You have been here for such a short time."

"We will be back," Carmen said. "We want to go to one of Agar's oceans and meet with the people who live in the water."

Sela closed her eyes for a moment, apparently concentrating on something.

"Yes. I see. Yes. That is also an important part of Agar. I have never communicated with the ocean dwellers. I will be interested in what you have to say when you return."

After all of the time the Agara have been in existence, and they haven't talked with the ocean dwellers. Just another unusual aspect of this unusual world, Carmen thought. She and Jesse left the village to teleport back to Thelika. Carmen thought that was better than teleporting right in front of the Agara.

When they got to the clearing where they had originally landed, and were ready to teleport, Jesse shouted, "Wait!"

"What is it?"

"We can't go back to Thelika, Carmen. We don't know if it's safe yet. We might contaminate Thelika. Then it would be stuck in our quarantine, too."

"You're right! We're so used to being able to go where we want to. We're going to have to be careful. What do we do now?"

"We'll have to ask Thelika to select a beach for us and send our stuff down there somehow."

* * *

Up in the tree shelter, Sam contacted Ahleeto through his implant.

"How are you doing up there?" he asked.

"Fine" Ahleeto answered. "Thelika and I are continuing the survey of the planet from orbit. We have used probes for a closer look at interesting sites. We're hoping the data we are compiling will be useful."

"I'm sure it will," Sam said.

"How are things on the surface?" Ahleeto asked

"Complicated. As you can tell from what we've been saying we may have become infected by a microorganism, which could have an undesirable effect on others. So we have to investigate the situation without leaving the planet surface. I will need your help and Thelika's, too."

"That explains the request we just received from Carmen and Jesse. They want Thelika to put together some equipment for swimming and send it to the surface. We are working on how to do that. In my state, I can't move things about. Thelika has some ability to do so, but it is limited."

"I'll also need some things sent to the surface. I think we need help. This has to be kept confidential, so it will have to be someone who knows how to work and keep quiet about it."

"Who do you have in mind?" Ahleeto asked.

"I've just thought of the perfect person—Travis Beckwith. His work with nano organisms and knowledge of the required equipment would be just the right combination. He could also help get things together to send to the surface. I'll connect with him and get back to you."

"Alright. I'll let Thelika know what is happening.

"Carmen?" Sam inquired through his implant.

"Yes, Sam," Carmen answered the same way.

"Thanks for remembering to not leave the surface. I'm going to get some help so we can get things to the surface, like your swim equipment. It shouldn't take long."

"We'll have Thelika pick a spot on the shore for us to go to. We'll wait there and look around while we are waiting."

"Perfect. I'll let you know when help has arrived."

* * *

Travis Beckwith, the head of nano research at Sunaj was in his office when Sam contacted him telepathically.

"Hi Sam. Where did you guys go?" Travis asked. *"When I asked Janus, he said you were off on some mysterious mission to a planet we hadn't heard of."*

"That's where we are, and we need your help."

Sam described the situation on Agar.

41

"Wow! That's hard to believe. Regeneration? Over an enormous time period? I'll take your word for it, but..."

"We have to keep this to ourselves until we know more."

"No problem. What do you need from me?"

"I need you to put together the equipment we need and come to the planet. I want you to work with me from orbit in Thelika while we do the analyses needed to find how the regeneration is accomplished and whether we are infected."

They talked about what equipment would be needed. Sam would need some on the surface, but most of it would be running on Thelika.

"Also, I need Martha to work with us. Please bring a copy of her with you."

"She'll love this."

"I think she will. Travis, we'll need you to do some fetch-and-carry work to send things to the surface for us. I would normally suggest additional staff to help us, but the fewer who know about this the better."

"Yes. I can see the complications. Don't worry. I can do what's needed."

"Good. I'll ask Ahleeto to bring Thelika to you."

Having done what he could, Sam sat back, and began designing the research project. He thought the Teratta might have useful information. Carmen had communicated most with the one she named Josh.

It was during those discussions the topic of regeneration had come up. It was Josh's comment that suggested that a microorganism might be at the center of the process, when he told Carmen, *"Parts of me stop functioning properly, but they are repaired, and I go on."* Sam knew he didn't need to be next to the tree to communicate with it, but right now he could use a walk. So he walked to the base of the tree he had climbed earlier.

"Josh?"

"Yes, Sam."

"I would like to know more about the process that sustains your life over the years."

"Why?"

Sam hadn't expected that response. Josh and their shelter tree had sounded so carefree when talking with them before. Josh sounded apprehensive now, concerned.

"I will gladly tell you, Josh, but is there something wrong?"

"We Teratta have been wondering what instigated your visit. We've had no visitors for our entire life. Then one space traveling ship comes, which Agar sends away, and then you arrive and are welcomed by Agar. We wonder why."

"So do we Josh. Do you think our visit has something to do with that earlier ship?"

"Only because the visits have occurred so close together."

Sam thought about that for a moment. He decided that a direct approach would be best. He was talking to a being who might be as old as life on Earth. Josh had a right to have his questions answered.

"There are two reasons I would like to know about the regeneration. First, we have been drawn here by some unknown Entity for a purpose we cannot fathom. That same Entity was the one who supplied you and Agar with information about us. We assume we are to learn as much as we can about Agar, and you who are part of Agar.

"Until we know more, we are working on the part we think we understand—learning about you and your planet. We are assuming that we will understand more of why we were asked to visit Agar at a later date."

"We are also interested in that. You said you have two reasons. What is the second reason?"

"Sustaining life of an organic being over the span of years that has occurred on Agar is unbelievable. What I mean is that

43

it does not occur that way on any other planet that we know of or can conceive of. We have a word for it. We would call you and the rest of life on Agar 'immortal,' which translates as does-not-die.

"*I recognize that dying or ending doesn't enter your conception of how things are, but it does everywhere else. If the means to become immortal were to be made available on other planets, they would be quickly overpopulated. Thus, we think that it should not be known that immortality exists here. We think that if it were discovered, you would be overrun with those who sought the secret.*"

"*How strange. Yet you have asked me for information about it. Should we be worried about you?*" Josh asked.

"*An excellent question, Josh. Many of my race would be among those who would seek out the source of your immortality. My companions and I need to know for another reason.*

We have been told by the Agara that by breathing Agar air or drinking Agar water, we have a part of Agar now in our body. We are concerned that if we left the planet, we would be carrying the seeds of immortality with us, and that it would spread to others on our planet, creating a population disaster. We want to understand how it works so that we can tell if it would be safe for us to leave your planet. If it isn't we will choose to stay here rather than spread it among our population."

"*You are so different from us,*" Josh said. "*After all this time with only ourselves to communicate with, the Teratta are now exposed to many new thoughts and a new feeling—concern. We have never been 'worried,' as I think you would say. We are not deeply worried, but the possibilities you raise do cause new thoughts to course through our being.*"

Sam was enjoying the discussion with Josh but wasn't sure where it would end. Would Josh and the Teratta help him, or not?

"I apologize if it distresses you." Sam said. *"We are not causing you this difficulty on purpose. We believe it is a result of our being drawn to visit you. We will learn about you, and you will learn about us. What we have to share is not all going to be a source of concern for you. Much of what we have to tell you could delight, or at least entertain you. There remains this one matter that we feel we have to clear up. Will you help us?"*

There was an unsettling, long pause before Josh replied. Sam wondered if it was because Josh was having difficulty making up his mind or because he had to check with the all the other Teratta on the planet before answering. The way his answer was phrased when it came sounded like it was the latter.

"Yes. The Teratta will help."

7. Unknown Waters

Thelika had selected a section of shoreline that was nearest the Agara village they had visited. Still, it was two hundred miles away. When they teleported there, Carmen and Jesse were struck by the calm waters and uniformity of the beach that went north and south of them for as far as they could see.

"This is more like a lake shore than an ocean beach," Jesse said.

The Teratta lined the shoreline nearly down to the water. Between the trees and the beach with its sand and small pebbles, was a nearly uniform-width, narrow border of the peat-like vegetation that seemed to cover most of the land surface.

"The vegetation stops just short of what must be the high tide line," Carmen said. "The tide doesn't seem to get very high. Also, there are no large boulders, or bluffs which have been eroded by the tides and storms. I agree it looks more like the shore of a lake within a forest. Still, looking out across the water there is no land visible on the other side."

She bent down and touched the water and then put her fingers to her lips.

"The water is moderately warm, at least near the shore. It's only slightly salty."

"Thelika, I forgot to check, does this planet have a moon?" Jesse asked.

"There is one, which is about one quarter the size of Earth's moon. By the way, I'll be leaving shortly to return to

46

Earth. I'll be picking up Travis and equipment. I don't think I'll be gone long. When I get back, Travis will be able to put your swim equipment together. Sorry for the delay."

"No problem," Jesse said. "Let us know when you return."

"It looks like we won't be going into the water for a while, Carmen. Shall we look around the local forest?"

She nodded and walked toward the trees. Walking a short distance into the forest, they stopped at a place where some sunlight made it to the forest floor and sat down with their backs to one of the trees.

"Hello and welcome."

They couldn't be sure which tree had greeted them. They assumed it was the one they were leaning against.

"Thank you," Carmen replied. *"Are you the tree we are leaning against?"*

"Yes, Carmen."

Carmen was only a little taken aback that this tree knew her name. She thought she'd explore that.

"Have all Teratta been listening to our conversations with the trees near the Agara village?"

"Yes, as you can imagine after all this time with no visitors to Agar, these exchanges are very interesting to all Teratta."

"Do you all communicate telepathically constantly?" Jesse asked.

"Yes."

"What about the Teratta on other land masses?"

"We are connected telepathically, Jesse, but until recently there was not anything new to discuss. We were delighted at the arrival of the new children in the Agara village you visited. They are such a novelty that the local Teratta keep the rest of us informed of their activities. The new young Agara are often climbing up and down the local Teratta.

"There are many more things to discuss now. The recent visit of the space vessel, which was encouraged to leave, was talked about long after it left. Then we were flooded with information about you and your arrival. Since you arrived thoughts have been racing around the globe. The discussion with local Teratta and your overheard conversations are floating through Teratta everywhere."

"How many Teratta are there on Agar?" Carmen asked.

"Nearly one hundred billion, to use your system of counting."

Carmen thought that was a very large number. Then she thought about the size of the land masses and that the Teratta were close to each other across all of it, and a hundred billion didn't seem to be large enough. She thought about the similarities and differences compared to the tree-like Cheneshi on Ocean. They too were connected telepathically.

She would have to explore that later. They were being contacted by Travis aboard Thelika, wondering what they wanted sent to the surface.

"Thank you for the discussion. We are going to prepare to go meet the people in the ocean."

"I'm not sure if you can communicate with them," the tree said. *"We have tried and were unsuccessful. Let us know how you fare."*

"We will."

Jesse and Carmen rose and went down to the shore again. They told Travis what was needed. He sent it down in one of Thelika's probes. They decided to keep the probe on the surface until the contamination possibilities were known. They changed into their swimsuits and flippers, adjusted weights, goggles, put their re-breathers into their mouths and waded into the water. By the time the water was up to their knees, they discovered that the water was refreshingly cool, but not cold. They were about to step further into the water, when a number of water creatures of indeterminate size began thrashing about in the water a short distance in front of them.

Jesse looked at Carmen.

"Fun or danger?"

"Well, they're keeping their distance so far, so we don't have to run away just yet. Let's try to communicate with them."

"Hello?" Carmen queried.

The thrashing stopped. The water became calm again. Carmen and Jesse stood still awaiting further developments. When none came, they took two more tentative steps away from the shore. They stopped again when a head rose out of the water where the thrashing was earlier.

"Are you the...?" the creature began, apparently not certain how to finish the question.

"We are the visitors on Agar," Carmen said.

"And you are coming into our water?"

"If we may, yes."

"We had the impression that you were land creatures. No one from the land comes into the water."

Carmen took the statement to mean that it was unheard of, not forbidden.

"We usually live on the land, but we can go into the water. We can't breathe underwater, so we have something to help us breathe when we are in the water."

The thrashing commenced again. Carmen and Jesse weren't sure how to interpret it. The explanation came when it stopped, and the head emerged from the surface again.

"Unusual, but yes, you may come into our water. Come. You will be safe. Nothing of Agar will bother you wherever you go."

Carmen and Jesse took their new host at its word. They slipped into the water and swam out toward where the activity was. Once submerged, they noticed that the water was exceptionally clear, except for the bit of sediment that had been stirred up by the four mer-people in front of them. They closely matched the description that Janus had provided. He had everything right but the size.

These creatures were nearly ten feet in length. Their head was round and about a foot across. Their body at the shoulder was over two feet in diameter. It became proportionately slimmer until it tapered and flattened to the single fin at the end. Their arms had webbed fingers at the end that were tipped with claws. Along the back of their body a spine was visible with a single dorsal fin about a third of the way down the body from the shoulder. There were what appeared to be gills on the short neck. The face was rounded, with wide-set eyes which had a lid that would cover them. The mouth was a thin slit which when opened displayed a set of sharp teeth.

"Greetings. My name is Heillan. Those with me are Trahan, Dracan and Sartra."

The others each nodded as they were named. All four had their eyes open in wonder at the new creatures before them.

"You have the legs of a land creature, but at the end is a fin like a water creature. Is that why you can go into both realms?"

"My name is Carmen and with me is Jesse. The fins are detachable."

Carmen demonstrated by bringing up one of her feet and taking the flipper off, and then replacing it. That caused their eyes to open even wider.

"Unusual," Heillan said, *"but then everything connected with your visit to Agar is unusual. Through Agar we were informed that there would be a visit. Then we were mysteriously informed all about you, including a language which had words for which we had no reference. Did you do all that informing before arriving?"*

"No. That is a mystery to us as well," Carmen said.

"Unusual. Yes, very unusual."

Carmen smiled at the thought that Heillan had learned a word in the Human language that he found useful.

"Come then. Swim and learn," Heillan said.

The four Agarians, as Carmen decided to call them until she found what they called themselves, took off at a speed the Humans could never match. They looked back at the visitors and swam back to them.

"We cannot swim that fast," Carmen said.

"We have a ways to go," Heillan said. *"Perhaps we could help you."*

A pair of Agarians swam to each of the Humans, so that Carmen and Jesse had an Agarian on their left and right sides. The Agarians gently put their webbed hand around the upper part of Jesse and Carmen's arms. That done, they both had two Agarian escorts, who led them rapidly through the water traveling near the ocean floor. The Agarians were gentle so that neither Carmen nor Jesse suffered under their care.

Along the way, they saw numerous other sea creatures, some swimming, some on the ocean floor. The shapes of the creatures were different than found on Earth, but given that they were living in the ocean, some similarities, like fins, were included and their shapes appeared functional.

Carmen studied their hosts while traveling. Before she thought she could guess the genders of the people in the Agara village, but she had no idea which was which among the swimmers carrying them along. Gender might not even be an issue for these creatures.

Just as she was beginning to worry that their hosts were going to take them to a depth that would kill them, they came to a monolithic structure that rose up two hundred feet from the ocean floor and was hundreds of feet wide.

It was a coral-like construction with numerous openings. There was light emanating from some of them. Their hosts led them up and over the outside wall of the structure and down into the central courtyard. There were numerous Agarians swimming around within the courtyard and outside of the structure as well. All the activity stopped when the Humans arrived at center-court. Then every Agarian in the vicinity swam at high speed directly at the new arrivals.

8. Something Familiar

"The Teratta will help," Josh had said. It was a simple statement, but with enormous implications. There were at least one hundred billion Teratta on Agar. One hundred billion creatures each millions of years old. Yes, that might be a lot of help.

Sam began to feel the Teratta's immense power from his short discussions with Josh. So how could he and Travis use this amazing resource? Sam had given Travis a briefing on how they came to Agar and what they had found when they arrived. Even so, he didn't think Travis would understand unless he came down to the surface, and that was not possible at this time. So they would work on the problem from two locations. He introduced Travis to Josh, and they began a three-way conversation.

"Josh, I appreciate your willingness to help us," Sam said. *"We need to answer several questions. What does the microorganism look like? Is it alive and operating within my body? Is there a danger that it could leave my body and go into another Human body?"*

"How do you plan to proceed?" Josh asked.

"We have instruments that will help us. We would start by looking at the microorganism in operation within part of Agar."

"What is a microorganism, Sam?"

"It is a name we would attach to what you think is inside of you repairing non-functioning parts. If we find what we are

looking for, we would like to see what it looks like and how it works. Comparing our conversations with you to the Agara in the village, I'm of the opinion that the Teratta have greater understanding of the regenerative process. So I'd like to learn from you."

"I think you are right, Sam. Those who call themselves Agara are relatively young. They believe that Agar does everything for them directly, rather than that there are, as you would say, chemical processes doing the work in the background. Can your instruments look inside of me, to watch the process?"

"Travis, what do we have?"

"I have sent you a portable scope that should be able to do the job. I have not used it in the field before. When everything is stable in a lab, the scope is usually easy to set up and get it focused. You'll just have to do the best you can. The probe needs to be inside a cell to view the DNA or probably RNA within Josh. It's quite a bit easier inserting it into the soft tissue of a Human. I sent it to you, because I thought it was what you needed, but I'm not sure that it will work. We are also assuming that cellular structure and genetic information are the same on this planet as on Earth."

"Oh, where would we be without assumptions to get us started?" Sam said

"Exactly."

"Josh, did you follow what we were proposing?"

"Yes, Sam. You will want to insert a very small instrument into me to look for the microorganism. I also understand that inserting it through my outer bark would be difficult. When you are ready, I will expose a small portion of my surface so that you will have access to softer material."

"Thank you."

Travis led Sam through the steps to get everything ready. Travis had sent down the equivalent of a small laboratory, including an enclosure. When it was set up next to Josh, Sam told Josh what needed to be done.

"As you can probably tell, Josh, I have set up a small structure right next to you. If you are ready, the next thing I will do is attach a short clean tube to your side. It will be about one foot in diameter. I know you don't know what that dimension is, but perhaps you will feel its size when I attach it."

"Go ahead and let me feel it."

Working from within the enclosure, Sam opened one of the clean-tubes and extended it to Josh's bark. It self-adhered to make an air-tight connection.

"I can feel it, Sam. Do you need that entire area exposed?"

"No. If you can open a part of that area at the center of the circle that will be enough."

Sam watched in amazement as the bark moved away from the center toward the edge exposing the soft inner fiber of the tree.

"That's it, Josh. I will be able to get the probe inside."

Sam felt like a doctor about to give a patient an injection when he said, *"The probe is very small like one of the needles on your branches, except longer and not as wide."*

"I don't think I will feel it. Go ahead."

Sam carefully moved the probe close to Josh and then eased it into the fibrous material. He was awed at the ability to see Josh's flesh at the cellular level on the screen of the instrument.

"Are you seeing this, Travis?"

"Yes, Sam."

"What do we do now? Should I insert the probe into one of the cells?"

"Let's wait a bit," Travis said. "We aren't sure if this process works inside the cells or works on them from the outside. Let's see if we can spot something unusual at work."

"Josh, what do you know about this process?"

"Only what we Teratta feel is going on, Sam. When we feel that some small part of us is not functioning properly, we feel that something takes care of it. We do not feel any of this unless we concentrate very intensely. Normally we just are alive and do not notice anything. I like the term microorganism. It seems like the right name for what we were sensing."

"Thanks, Josh."

"Travis why don't Humans regenerate and live forever?"

"Instead of thinking about the inside of us for that question, for our work here let's think about what it looks like on the outside when we become aged. If nothing went wrong on the inside, we would continue to look young on the outside, but we don't. Skin, bone, eyes, hair, those cells are no longer what they were earlier. They aren't 'young' anymore. Something changes in the cellular reproduction to start producing cells that no longer are as functional as the original design."

"So Josh continues to look like he always has because he isn't reproducing bad cells?" asked Sam.

"Seems like a good idea to pursue, Sam. So what's keeping Josh from producing bad cells?" Travis asked.

"Something inside him is eliminating cells that are no longer of the original design," Sam conjectured. "Is that all there is to it?"

"Let's look for the elimination process, and see if other things are going on," Travis said.

They concentrated on their respective screens. They saw Josh's cells and the fluid in between them, undoubtedly doing the same thing that the fluid between cells does in plants and animals on Earth. Sam and Travis spotted the anomaly at the same time. Moving in the fluid between the cells was a small sphere which was covered with small hairs.

"What's that?" Sam asked.

"It may be what we are looking for," Travis said. "It looks very familiar to me, but we'll deal with that issue later. Let's watch what it does as it moves around among the cells."

As they watched, the sphere slowed near a cell that had a slightly different shape.

"It looks like there is something wrong, or at least different about the cell that the sphere stopped by," Sam said.

They continued to watch the sphere. It attached itself to the cell using its hairs. Then in the area where the sphere was attached, the cellular wall was breached. The sphere moved away. The contents and wall of the cell dissolved into the fluid.

As Sam and Travis watched another irregularly shaped cell was broken into by a sphere that came floating through.

"Is that the regeneration process, Travis?" Sam asked. "Is getting rid of dysfunctional cells all that is required?"

"I would hesitate to make such a claim on so little evidence, Sam, but it certainly seems to be a necessary part of the process. We may not learn whether it's sufficient by itself to get the whole job done. Let's take a look at your insides, Sam. Let's see if the same furry sphere is in fact within you."

Sam retracted the probe and clean tube from Josh and thanked him. He then attached a new probe to the instrument, cleaned a spot on his arm, and inserted the probe into his arm. They waited quite a while but saw nothing. He removed the probe. He cleaned a spot on his thigh and inserted the probe. After a longer wait, they still did not see the sphere.

"I've only breathed in the air and drunk the water," Sam said. "Perhaps if I had ingested some local food I might have some spheres inside me."

"That might be the case," Travis said. "It might also take time for the spheres to develop within your body. Let's do this testing again after you've been on the surface for a while. We'll also check Carmen and Jesse when they get back. We could test your theory about the food, but I don't think it's a good idea. If you are clean after breathing and drinking, I think we should leave it at that."

"So that's it?" Sam asked.

"For now, yes." Travis said. "We'll do the other tests I mentioned later. There's something else I want you to take a look at."

"What did you find out, Sam?" Josh asked.

"That you were right. There does seem to be something inside you which eliminates cells which are no longer healthy. So the Teratta feelings about this are confirmed."

"You can't possibly understand what that confirmation means to us, Sam. We have been conjecturing about this topic for a very long time with no way to find out if what we thought was in fact the way of things. From all the Teratta, thank you."

"You're welcome, Josh. Thank you for letting us use you in our investigation. I think we'll be working together on other things during my stay here."

"We look forward to it."

Sam put things in the mini lab back together but didn't shut it down completely. What Travis wanted to show him might need the equipment.

"I'm ready, Travis. What do you have?" Sam asked.

"Look at your scope. I recorded what we saw inside Josh. I'm going to let it run until we can see the sphere clearly. Then I'm going to split the screen and show you another shot."

Sam watched as Travis' presentation unfolded. A sphere came on the screen and was frozen in place. Then the screen split, and another picture was put up. It also had a sphere in it. It looked exactly like the one they found in Josh.

"They look the same."

"I agree," Travis said.

"Where did the photo of the other sphere come from?"

"From inside the testicle of a Human male. In Human males, this sphere is performing the function of creating H2 DNA. I am reluctant to jump to conclusions. After all, this is a very useful design for doing work at a nano level. Even viruses on Earth have a shape very similar to this."

"Similar, but not exactly the same, whereas the two spheres before us look alike."

"Sam I have done some quick graphical analysis and measurement. They are exactly the same. They've been programmed to perform different functions. I can't prove it, so I won't claim they came from the same source."

"But if they have...."

"Yes, Sam if they have, if they have...what does that mean?"

9. Summoned

Carmen and Jesse needn't have worried about the stampede of Agarians. They were only racing to make sure they could get a spot where they could see the visitors. Of course the Humans didn't know that until the swimmers stopped abruptly when they arrived and began asking questions. Heillan took charge of the chaos.

"They cannot answer all your questions at the same time. I've heard most of your questions during our discussions when we learned that they had arrived. Let me try to speak for all of us. I'm sure you will let me know if I missed something."

They wanted to know where Carmen and Jesse were from, why they were on Agar, and if they were the ones who provided the information that allowed them to learn the Human language. Carmen and Jesse did their best to answer the questions. Their audience was confused when they didn't have answers to some of them. Heillan summed up after a short time.

"You were asked to come here, but you do not know why. You think at least part of the reason you are here is to learn about Agar and all of us. What would you like to know about us?"

Carmen wanted to know several things. One in particular was whether the Agarians were immortal. She thought that she would hold off on that. Jesse started off with a less controversial question.

"Are there others like you in other parts of the ocean?"

"Yes. Each group lives in a structure like this one."

Carmen could guess the answer to her next question but asked it anyway.

"How was this structure created?"

"Agar grew it, from the ocean bottom."

"What do you call yourselves?"

"We have not called ourselves anything. Those in the village on land call themselves the Agara, the people of Agar. We are people of Agar, but we do not want to call ourselves the same thing as them."

"How about Agarians?" Carmen offered.

Heillan looked around at the other Agarians. They all seemed agreeable to that name.

"That is a wonderful name, Carmen. We accept."

Carmen enjoyed filling the name void but wondered how they could have gone so long without naming themselves. Humans seemed to have a need to put a name on everything. These people seemed to be fine just existing as they are without a name.

"Will the others of your kind agree with the name?" Jesse asked.

Heillan hesitated for a moment. Apparently like the Teratta and the Agara, the Agarians were connected telepathically across the globe. Heillan said as much when he answered.

"Every one of the Agarians is fine with the new name. Actually they were very happy to have been given a name. They all thank you for your gift, Carmen."

Carmen was curious about something else. Especially since the Agarians knew what the villagers called themselves.

"The Teratta close to the shore where we entered the water said that they have tried to communicate with you but have received no answer."

"Yes. That is true."

When Heillan didn't explain, Carmen pursued it further.

"Why didn't you respond?"

"We have occasionally listened in on their communications. What they talk about does not interest us. The Teratta talk about Teratta things. The Agara talk about villager things. We have not seen the need to learn about things outside of the water."

Carmen thought Humans would feel they had to know what was going on elsewhere. The Cheneshi on Ocean certainly had developed a comprehensive knowledge of their planet. The people on Agar were fine with only knowing about their part. Carmen found the contrast interesting. Jesse must also have felt it odd. His next question sounded a little rude to Carmen, but it didn't seem to bother the Agarians. She was glad he asked it. She thought it was fundamental to understanding the people of Agar.

"What do you do?" Jesse asked.

Heillan looked at Jesse with what Carmen took to be a quizzical expression.

"Do? What do you mean?"

"Most Humans have what we call an occupation. For example, Carmen's occupation is one that studies the ways of other people, such as the Agarians. She spends time during most days doing that."

"Do you enjoy doing that Carmen?"

"Yes."

Heillan looked relieved.

"Then we are the same. What we do, Jesse is we do what we enjoy. We swim in the ocean, look at the interesting things around us, and we eat."

Carmen was piecing together a picture of life on Agar but wasn't carving it in stone. She had seen so little of the planet. Still, some things seemed to be clear. She finally needed to address a sensitive issue and thought of a way to do it.

"Heillan, in the village we visited we were told that Agar made the two children that are there because two of the villagers had ended. Has anything happened to have one of you end like that?"

Heillan's eyes became wider and wider as Carmen added to her story. His face ended in a shocked expression when she was done. It looked like he was having a difficult time responding.

"I did not know that something so terrible had happened to the villagers. I should have realized something had happened when two new, small villagers appeared. No, Carmen, nothing so tragic has happened in our memory, which extends over a very long time. We Agarians do not end."

Carmen thought she had the final data she needed to knit together her tentative description of life on Agar, and it was an "unusual" story, to use Heillan's favorite word. Although she had what she needed, she thought it would be very rude of her to just ask to be returned to the beach. She looked at Jesse to see if he had additional questions. He shook his head, so she took the next step.

"Thank you so much for helping us learn about you. Do you have other questions you would like to ask us?"

They had many questions. Carmen and Jesse did their best to answer them. Like the Teratta and the Agara, the Agarians were given information about their Human visitors from an unknown source. The Agarians wanted to know what many of the words and other data meant. They had even less of a reference for the concepts than the other two groups since Humans were land animals and the Agarians were not. They seemed to be delighted each time something new was explained. Many swam around excitedly as the first four had when they saw the Humans wade into the water.

Finally, when the questioning seemed to have ended, Carmen and Jesse said their goodbyes to the Agarians and requested that Heillan and the others return them to the beach. Carmen and Jesse could have teleported there, but she thought doing something so strange in front of the Agarians would not be a good idea.

When they were returned to the beach, they slipped shorts and tops over their swimwear. They walked into the forest so the Agarians wouldn't see them, and then teleported to the spot near Josh.

They saw the equipment Sam had been using. Sam wasn't there. When they contacted him they learned he was in their assigned shelter. They walked into the village, up the tree, and into their shelter. Sam was sitting on one of the platforms. Carmen and Jesse sat down on the other two. It was time to assess the results of the two separate investigations.

"Before we begin," Carmen said, "we should keep in mind that at least the Teratta are listening in. I don't think the others are, but we can't know for sure."

"Does that make a difference?" Sam asked.

"I'm not sure it does. For me, I will be talking about life on Agar. I will want to keep from offending the life that is listening. On the other hand it could be that the Teratta could comment on our conclusions. Shall we invite our home tree to take an active role?"

In response to Carmen's question, Sam asked, *"Josh, can you overhear our conversation from where we are?"*

"Yes, Sam. So can the tree you are housed within. In fact you have most of the attention of all Teratta at this point. If it is easier for you to think of conversing with me, then use my new name."

"Thank you, Josh. We are not used to carrying on a conversation with one hundred billion individuals. We are about to start a discussion of what we have learned in our short time on Agar. We would appreciate it if you would listen in. We would like you to comment on our discussion when you

64

think it would be appropriate. We'll be conversing verbally, so let us know if you miss something and would like us to repeat it."

"Thank you for including us."

Sam began by telling Carmen and Jesse what he and Travis learned.

"So we aren't contagious?" Jesse asked.

"It's too early to be sure, but it doesn't seem like we are. We will want to probe all three of us as a final check."

"That's encouraging," Carmen said. "If we're ready to move on, I'd like to ask you a question, Josh."

"What is it Carmen?"

"Do the Agara eat food to sustain their lives? It may seem like an unnecessary question, but we haven't been here long enough to observe their habits."

"Yes. That is their way. They sometimes eat plants, though I think that they get most of their sustenance from drinking Agar's water."

"May I ask how you know that?" Jesse asked.

"It is from monitoring their thoughts since they emerged to become part of Agar."

"Do you also monitor the people in the ocean, and is it the same with them?"

"Yes, to both of your questions, Jesse. To answer your next question, the Teratta get all of their sustenance through our roots and sunlight striking our branches."

"We have talked about death and decay as being part of life on Earth. The food consumed by the Agara and the ocean people who we gave the name Agarians, stops being what it was and becomes part of them," Carmen said.

"Yes. Those parts of Agar that are food for the people do end."

"We noticed plants near the clearing where we landed which looked like small trees. They had what we would call leaves which dropped off of them. I imagine that those leaves are absorbed into the ground to return to Agar. Do those small trees decay and die like their leaves?"

"Yes. Most plants and creatures on Agar go through that process. The Teratta do not."

"Thank you for the clarification."

She paused, gathering her thoughts.

"Well, team, we've been on Agar less than one whole day, and have seen only a small part of the globe. It is too early to make conclusive statements about life on this planet. Still, there appears to be some uniformity. The Teratta, Agara and Agarians seem to be the same across the planet, and all of them can be in contact with each other. Perhaps we can tentatively say that what we have learned from the few we have talked with describes the situation for the others.

"What have we found? That there are three races on the planet, which are all basically immortal, because of a regeneration process that repairs any part of them that stops working properly. The Teratta have been in place since major life forms existed on Agar. The Agara and Agarians are more recent arrivals and are merely hundreds of thousands of years old.

"This is truly an unusual and very likely a unique expression of life in the universe!" Carmen said.

"Good summary, Carmen." Sam said. "I think we need to ask ourselves if we think this is a sufficient level of knowledge. Do we need to know more to carry out the mission we have apparently been assigned?"

"I do not know the requirements of your mission," Josh said, *"but I believe you will gain a deeper understanding of Agar by spending more time with the Teratta. In particular the First Teratta, the eldest of our kind, request your presence."*

10. Point of Origin

Sam told Josh that they would be honored to meet with the First Teratta. It was getting late. The sun was beginning to set. He asked if they could meet with the elders the next day. Josh said that the First Teratta agreed.

On their way out of the village Carmen stopped to tell Sela that they would be leaving. Sela smiled, nodded and went back to her work. Since Sela didn't seem to require any further information Carmen didn't offer any. She walked away and caught up with Sam and Jesse.

They went where the mini lab was set up near Josh. They wanted to go back to Thelika but needed to test themselves first. When they found no evidence of the microorganism in any of their bodies, they decided it was safe to return to the ship.

They packed the equipment back into the probe and asked Thelika to retrieve it and the one they left at the beach by sending a return signal to each probe. Then, away from the village, Sam, Jesse and Carmen teleported themselves back to the ship. They took time to wash and change clothes before meeting with Travis and Ahleeto in the common room for an evening meal.

"Quite an adventure," Travis said. "How did all of this start?"

Sam asked Janus to tell Travis about the experience Janus had been having with an unknown Entity. When Janus was done, Carmen told Travis and Ahleeto about their early findings about life on Agar.

"So population is held to a certain level," Travis said, "and when the two Agara were lost, they were replaced to bring the Agara population back to its original number."

"Yes," Carmen said. "We don't know how the new ones were produced. I wish I would have asked Josh if he knew."

"Why don't you ask him now?" Travis asked.

"Good idea. I hadn't thought of that."

"Josh, do the Teratta know how the new Agara were made?"

"How interesting, Carmen. You are contacting me from your vessel above the planet. We have never experienced that before."

"I'm glad it works. Do you know the answer?"

"Yes, though I don't think it will help. Agar made them."

Carmen looked at those around her, a bit exasperated.

"You are right, Josh. I would like more information. Do you know where they first appeared?"

"Yes. On the ground not far from me."

"Did they just appear out of the air?"

"No. I think it would be more accurate to say they appeared out of the ground."

"Could you explain that?"

"Though we could not see it happen, we felt the ground in motion, rising up in an area near me. When the motion stopped the next sensation we experienced was movement on top of that part of the ground, steps like the Agara, but lighter. Then we began to sense thoughts—immature, not fully-formed. Then the steps went toward the village."

Carmen and the others were struck dumb. After a prolonged silence, Josh interrupted their silence.

"Carmen, did you understand my explanation?"

"Yes, Josh. We think we understood what happened. It is just totally outside of our experience, and we are having trouble absorbing it. I'll be back to you in a minute."

"Lose two? Grow two!" Travis said. "Simple, but...."

"Up out of the ground?" Jesse asked. "How could that be?"

"Josh, is that how the original Agara appeared on the surface?"

"Yes, Carmen, now that you mention it, that was how they appeared. It was very long ago, which explains why we did not recognize the process when the two new ones arrived. Yes. That is how it was, and they were small like these two at first. Thank you for reminding us."

"And the people in the ocean?"

"I cannot be sure, but I believe that is how Agar produced them as well. The ocean bottom is so far from the Teratta that we could not sense the ground movement from their arrival. We did sense the growth of the structures they live in, and we sensed the thoughts of the Agarians as you have named them— immature at first as were those of the Agara."

"Thank you, Josh."

"Anyone have words to describe how extraordinary this is?" Sam asked. "I do not."

"It is beyond anything the Lorengi discovered in their search for life on planets," Ahleeto said. "Janus, in trying to communicate with the planet, have you found out more about Agar?"

"Not much more than I have already described," Janus answered through their implants. "Agar does not appear to be able to communicate anything more than feelings. I think that those feelings can be frightfully strong, but they do not communicate any detail. I find it odd that Agar has created beings that are able to communicate with us, but Agar itself cannot."

"Like Sam, I don't have the vocabulary to describe or discuss the phenomenon that is Agar," Jesse said. "Perhaps we can talk about the physical planet itself. What have you and Thelika learned, Ahleeto?"

"The three large landmasses are remarkably similar in shape and size. The center of each landmass is located one-hundred-twenty degrees from the center of the others. The oceans in between them are connected by wide passages between the land and the ice at the poles. There is one small moon, which creates modest tides. There is no perceptible tip in Agar's axis. Because of that and its location relative to the sun, the planet experiences a uniform season all year long, similar to a warm spring on Earth. The rainstorm you experienced occurs around the globe, at different times locally, with a high degree of regularity. There do not appear to be tropical storms, tornadoes, or other major storms like Earth experiences.

"One other thing that warrants attention is that the Teratta are not densely packed on land. They have space between them that allows sunlight to reach the ground in between them with some large areas left open."

"Thelika, do you have instruments that can measure the structure of the planet?"

"Yes, Travis. You have wondered if this planet is a very large artifact. I wondered about that too, and I did some deep probing. Agar appears to have a structure similar to Earth's but there are interesting differences.

The crust of Agar is thicker and more uniform than that of Earth and contains abundant naturally occurring deposits of heavy metal ores, as well of ores that would be considered rare on Earth. There are no magma intrusions anywhere near the surface. There is no evidence of historic volcanism."

"Stable planet and climate, symmetrical land formations, uniform vegetation dispersion, and immortal, self-regenerating sentient beings that emerge from the planet and have fixed populations. Did I miss anything?" Travis asked.

"No, Travis," Sam said. "I think you have summarized what we know so far. I believe that when we learn more about the planet we will likely find more evidence of thoughtful planning."

"That information download is beginning to make more sense."

"What do you mean, Jesse?" Travis asked.

"When we went to the surface, we learned that Agar had been given information about us that allowed the sentient races to know about us, our arrival and to communicate with us."

"Where did that come from?" Travis asked.

"We are assuming that it came from the same Entity that has been communicating with me and requested that we came to Agar," Janus said.

"I agree that is likely," Jesse said, "but I wasn't thinking about the source. I was wondering about the mechanism for absorbing that information. Apparently Agar received it and then added it to the knowledge of the sentient beings. The planet seems to be functioning as if it has been programed. If we think of the planet that way then the Teratta, Agara, and Agarian are subsystems, and they were given an 'update.'"

"Interesting concept," Travis said. "It's easier to imagine if I think of it in those terms."

The others nodded their understanding of what Jesse's comment suggested. They talked more about the unusual planet below them. They finished their meal and went to their cabins.

The next morning, they prepared to go to the surface again. This time Ahleeto and Travis were going with the others. They contacted Josh to see if he could give them directions to where the First Teratta were.

Josh suggested that they look for a small grove of trees near the middle of the land he was on. The cluster would be separated from the other Teratta by a large clear area surrounding it. Thelika did the search and found a cluster like that on each of the three landmasses. They focused on the one on Josh's land.

The grove of trees was roughly circular and about nine-hundred feet in diameter. There was a clear band sixty feet in width of what looked like grassland surrounding the cluster. There was another clearing about thirty feet in diameter at the center of the cluster. They teleported to the clear band of grassland outside the cluster.

"Welcome, travelers, I see there are more today than yesterday—one more Human, and an insubstantial being of a different race."

"I am Ahleeto, a Lorengi. Am I speaking with the First Teratta?"

"You are. I am the one directly in front of you."

To orient themselves, the group walked to the tree they thought was addressing them. Jesse put his hand on it.

"Are you this one?"

"Yes, Jesse. Would you like to climb upon me?"

"Maybe later."

"We have come as you asked," Sam said, "and are eager to talk with you. We think that part of the reason we have been summoned is to learn about you and all of Agar. We are pleased to have the opportunity. Beyond that we aren't sure why we are here."

"Yes, yes. We also do not know the reason for your visit, but we wanted to talk with you. Agar wanted to communicate with you and may use us to accomplish that. So we thought it best that you come to the Center of Origin. Please come into our cluster and go to the center."

'Center of Origin'? Agar wanted to 'communicate' with them? Carmen wondered what this was all about. Maybe they would find out once they were in the center.

The First Teratta were somewhat closer to each other than the other Teratta, but filtered sunlight still reached the ground between them. It took only a few minutes to reach the center. Immediately upon entering the center clearing, Carmen had a feeling of awe permeate her. There was a sense of immense age and deep calm. She looked at the rest of the team and it appeared they were having similar feelings. One of the trees next to where they entered the clearing modified its shape to create a bench for them to sit on. The Humans sat down, but Ahleeto's image remained standing next to them.

"Thank you," Carmen said. "Shall we assume we are talking with you?"

"Yes," their bench host said, *"if it makes you more comfortable."*

"It does help us to assume we are talking with an individual."

The team looked at each other wondering what to do next. Travis took the initiative.

"We find your world, unusual," Travis said, "or at least different from our planet and others we are familiar with. Life seems to follow a different path on each planet where it exists, but it is always a random path with life showing up spontaneously in different forms in different locations. Life on your planet seems to be planned, following a pre-set pattern."

"Yes."

"Can you explain why that is?"

"No."

Carmen thought asking additional questions like Travis had just asked might not get them anywhere.

"What did you want to discuss with us?" she asked.

"We are curious, and Agar is curious about what you have discovered as you have explored the planet. You are our first visitors. We wondered if you could tell us about ourselves."

11. Agar

Carmen was surprised by the request. By the looks on their faces, her companions were too. Their look was also an invitation for her to take this one.

"You hesitate, Carmen?" one of the Teratta around them inquired.

"Only because we are a little confused by your request. Of course we will tell you all we think about Agar. Our confusion is that to us, you are very long-lived, and we associate long life with knowledge and wisdom. So we were expecting to learn from you."

"Perhaps we can learn from each other."

"That is a very good idea," Carmen said. "Let me begin with our assessment. Then you can ask questions about it."

"Yes."

"As Travis said, this planet and the life on it look as if it is following a plan. There is symmetry in the landmasses that the Teratta live on. Land on other planets has random shapes and locations. The climate is apparently controlled to support life and avoid damaging storms. The climates on other planets can be chaotic and severe. The Teratta, Agara and the people in oceans we named Agarians live without end through a process we would call regeneration and have a fixed population. On other planets, all life has an end, and is replaced with new life. The population of all plants and animals continues to increase until it runs into a limit of some sort, such as shortage of sustenance, then the population levels off. The order and symmetry of your planet and the life on it, give us the impression that it was planned from the beginning by some intelligence.

"All three sentient races on Agar are telepathic. That is not common. Your planet is a live organic being. On most other planets, life is made up of individual units of plant and animal life, all interdependent, but not consolidated into one living, organic being like the situation here. You were given information about us, which was assimilated by the others. Nothing like that has occurred on any other planet that we are aware of.

"In summary, your planet and the life on it are unique and astounding. We would be very interested to know how you came into being. In particular, why were the Teratta, Agara, and Agarians given sentience, and eternal life? We do try to extend our lives, but only can by a small margin. We wouldn't know what to do after a few hundred years, yet you are apparently not troubled by your long lives. From your answer to one of our questions, we have the impression that you do not know how all this came about."

"Thank you, Carmen. You have given us a wonderful gift, an outside perspective on our existence. You are right. We do not know how it all came about. Until we learned of you, and you came and talked with us, we assumed our way of life was normal.

"The Teratta and our planet are troubled. We do not think the Agara and Agarians are. We understand that our way is our way, but now that we know that others exist on different planets, and that their way is more like yours, we feel...vulnerable."

"I can understand how it might be disturbing to you, but your way of things has been working for a very long time," Carmen said. "Our way is just different, not better, certainly not better for you. The program that seemingly guides existence on Agar is fine for you."

Carmen looked at her companions and asked, "Is this why we are here, to protect them?"

"Sounds plausible," Sam said. "What do you think, Janus?"

"I think it might be the reason. The planet may be able to defend itself, but we don't know what it might be up against. It could be the Entity that brought us here intended that we become aware of this vulnerability."

"I have a question that might help," Sam said. "Can the Teratta tell me about the space vessel that came close to your planet earlier? We understand that the planet didn't like it and caused it to leave somehow. Why didn't Agar like it?"

"Our planet had the impression that those on the vessel wanted to dig, cut, and take things away."

The group on the bench looked at each other with a tentative expression of understanding.

"We have been wondering why we were asked to come here," Sam said. "Perhaps it is to help you with other visitors somehow?"

"We don't know, Sam, but we think we need help. If you were guided here for that reason, we welcome your help."

"We need to know more about you. It could be that part of the answer would come from understanding your beginning. Is there any way to investigate that? "

"Not that we know of."

"You have brought us to this location to discuss this," Sam continued. "This is the Point of Origin for the Teratta race. Is there something unusual about this part of the planet?"

"We don't know. Perhaps with your instruments, you could determine that."

"Ahleeto, what do you and Thelika think? Is there something unusual here? Is there some reason that whoever set all this up began here?"

"Thelika, could you focus on this spot?" Ahleeto asked. "I don't know what we are looking for, but anything anomalous would be of interest."

Thelika took a few minutes to answer.

"I hadn't noticed it before, but the surface temperature in the area that you are standing on is one point five degrees warmer than the surrounding area. As I probe deeper, the temperature gradient is higher as well. I've discovered a chamber sixty feet below the surface which appears to be the source of the heat. I cannot tell whether it is a natural phenomenon or artificial. The chamber is about forty feet wide and thirty feet in height."

"Examine similar spots on the other landmasses," Ahleeto said.

A few minutes later Thelika had the answer.

"There appear to be chambers at all three locations."

"That seems to point to artificial structures," Travis said.

"I'm thinking the same thing," Sam said. "Getting into the chamber below us might yield some of the answers we are looking for."

"We don't know what's there," Jesse said. "Teleporting into the chamber might prove to be a serious mistake."

"Thelika, can you assess the conditions within the interior of the chamber below us?"

"Not accurately, Sam. I believe the interior temperature is seventy-five degrees Fahrenheit. I cannot determine if there is air inside, or if there is, whether it is breathable."

"Aside from temperature and air, if it is an artificial chamber, it might be set to protect itself from intruders," Carmen cautioned.

"I do not have to worry about breathing, Carmen," Ahleeto said, "and I do not think safeguards against intruders will harm me. I'll go and see what is there."

"That would be a great help, Ahleeto" Sam said. "Be careful."

Ahleeto nodded.

"Thelika, can you direct me to a vacant space within the chamber?"

"Yes, Excellency."

A moment later, Ahleeto was gone from the surface, and found herself in a room which was lit only by lights on an instrumentation panel along the walls of the chamber.

"Intruder, identify yourself!" demanded a voice that seemed to come from everywhere in the room. "Tell me why you are worthy to enter this space. Be quick if you desire continued existence."

Ahleeto said. "I am Ahleeto Antilos, daughter of the Queen of the Lorengi. Who are you to threaten me?"

"Pardon my abrupt manner, Queen-Daughter. I meant no disrespect. In this strange new language I have been given I believe it would be appropriate to call me Agar."

"Rest easy, Agar. I am not offended."

"Thank you. Again, I mean no disrespect, but you do not seem to be a real person. I have been informed of visitors, but they were to be Humans, not Lorengi."

"I am an emissary of the Humans. They wanted to determine if the air within your chamber was the same as it is on the surface. I volunteered to come first. As to my form, I have been stored digitally, and have projected myself into your location."

"It was said that the Urritan stored themselves in a similar way," Agar said. "I have no confirmation that they did. It was a long time ago. You may assure the Humans the conditions are the same here as on the surface, and that I eagerly await their visit. Wait, how will they get into this chamber? There are no entrances."

"They will teleport into this chamber."

"Ah, just as the Urritan did."

"I will return in a moment with the Humans."

Ahleeto returned to the surface and told them about her experience in the chamber. They had numerous questions but understood that Agar would be the right one to answer them. Sam thought it appropriate to keep their surface hosts informed.

"There is what we would call a cyber-based intelligence within the chamber below," he told the Teratta. "We will ask it some of our questions."

"An intelligence below the surface? How can that be? To what purpose?"

"We will return and tell you what we have learned."

"Thank you, Sam."

The group teleported into the dark chamber below the surface. When they arrived, the lights in the room came on, apparently in response to the physical presence of Humans, something that Ahleeto's presence hadn't triggered.

"There are four of you with Queen-Daughter, Ahleeto," Agar said. "Are you four Human?"

Even with the lights on, it wasn't obvious where Agar's voice was emanating from. The walls of the chamber were all made of some kind of bronze colored metal. Various instruments had small colored indicator lights on, some blinking.

"Yes, my name is Sam. With me are Carmen, Jesse and Travis."

Knowing that they were likely being viewed each raised a hand when their name was called.

"Why have you come to this planet, Sam?"

"We do not know. We thought we might be able to determine the answer to that question by talking with you."

"Odd. You have come here, and do not know why?"

"Ahleeto tells us that you were told we would be coming and were given knowledge about us which allows you to communicate with us," Sam said. "We believe that the same Entity that gave you that knowledge asked us to travel to this planet without telling us why.

"We felt it was important. So we came. I think we are meant to help in some way, though you seem to have everything operating well. Can you tell us more about yourself and this planet? We might jointly begin to understand why we were asked to come here."

"Yes. To begin with the name the Urritan gave this planet is not Agar. They called it Perillian. When the Entity communicated with me we translated my function on this planet as best we could into your language. I am one, cyber intelligence in three identical locations on the planet. In your language I perform Administration, Guidance and Repair functions for this planet. Thus I was given the acronym AGAR as a name. I informed the sentient beings on the surface that this was my name translated into your language."

While that astounding bit of news settled in, the team looked around the circular space they were in. There were several workstations set against the walls. The chairs that sat before them had a shape that would be suitable for Humans, but they were four feet above the floor of the chamber and much wider than would be required for the Human anatomy.

"Were the Urritan, large people?"

"Yes, Jesse. The Urritan were nearly twice your height. They had two legs and two arms, but they were much bigger all around in proportion to their greater height."

"This planet looks like it was created, or at least shaped. Did the Urritan do this?"

"Yes, Travis. They shaped it into a form suitable for their purpose."

"What was their purpose?" Carmen asked.

"It was to be a garden planet for them to visit. Although once it was created, the Urritan never returned."

"How long ago was that?" asked Carmen.

"In your system of counting, two million years, which I believe is about the same in the years of your home planet."

Carmen thought about their original assumption about the age of the Teratta, but the difference really didn't matter. Two-million years of regeneration was still a long time to live.

"Were the Teratta sentient when they were first introduced?"

"No, Carmen. That happened much later. I'm not sure what triggered their self-awareness, but it began to appear about one million years ago."

"What about the others?"

"After millennia without input from the Urritan, I created the others. They were imbued with self-awareness from the beginning. The Agara turned out to be gentle, simple people, but not very playful. I added a bit more playfulness in the demeanor of the latest children I created. Those you named Agarians, were very playful from the beginning."

"You created, living sentient beings?" Jesse asked. "No wonder they think of you as some sort of all-knowing being which provides for their needs."

"You might think of them as more like automatons. They are alive and they think, but I programed their brains, and am still in communication with them. The Teratta, on the other hand, have evolved into self-aware beings on their own."

"The Teratta aren't alone in that," Janus said. *"The planet has begun the early stages of self-awareness."*

Agar did not respond right away. When it did, some of its former confidence and self-assurance had disappeared.

"Whoever and wherever you are, are you certain of this?"
"Yes."

12. New Friends

"Who was that?" Agar asked. "It spoke to me as the Urritan did all those years ago. No one has communicated to me like that since then. Is an Urritan with you?"

Carmen said. "We can all communicate that way."

"You can? Then that was one of you?"

"Not, exactly. Let me explain."

Carmen told Agar about Janus.

"Amazing. You can move like the Urritan. You can communicate like them. What is this about the planet becoming self-aware?"

"It is something that Janus detected when we first arrived."

Carmen thought that Agar seemed shaken. She surmised it might be that before this announcement it felt like it was in control of everything related to this planet. Planet self-awareness was not something it could fit into that previous reality.

"How could this happen?" Agar asked.

"I can only guess," Carmen said. "On the surface of this planet there are one-hundred billion, self-aware Teratta. That much self-awareness touching the planet might have triggered the same thing in the rest of the planet. Another question might help. Did you notice when another space-faring ship came into the system?"

"Yes," Agar said. "It seemed to probe the surface, and then left abruptly."

"That is all you know of the event?" Carmen asked.

"Yes."

"There was more to the event than that." Carmen said. "The Teratta told us that they had the feeling that 'Perillian' didn't like the vessel, and made it go away. They said that it sensed that the people on the ship wanted to 'dig and cut and take things away.' As far as we know the planet cannot communicate anything but feelings yet. We cannot predict if it will ever get beyond that, but it is awake."

Agar didn't respond right away. Jesse took the opportunity to walk toward one of the workstations. He hopped up into the chair and found that he couldn't reach the controls. His arms weren't long enough.

"This was unforeseen," Agar said, as if talking to itself.

"I think we have a foundation for discussion of our situation now," Sam said. "I am beginning to get the idea that something sensed the situation here and the potential threat. I don't know what we can do about it, but the Entity seems to have brought us here to try to help protect 'Perillian' from exploitation.

"After eons of isolation from the rest of the galaxy, apparently the planet has been discovered. Thelika's probes of the planet found that the crust is rich in mineral deposits. To an uninformed outsider, even the Teratta might look like a valuable resource. They would see the forests of Perillian as an untouched source of wood of amazing value.

"Agar, do you have any defensive weapons?"

Agar didn't respond. Sam looked at the others. Jesse had hopped back down and came over to the group.

"As you said, Sam, what can we do?" Travis asked.

Sam repeated his question to Agar. This time he received a response.

"No, Sam, I have no weapons of any kind." The planet manager sounded dejected. His well-ordered, millions-of-years existence had been disrupted severely.

"Don't worry, Agar. We have ways to respond."

"Things have changed forever, Sam. I do not know what it means. It is not just the possible outside threat. It is…things have changed."

"We will need your help, Agar. Whatever we come up with, I'm sure you will have an important role to play. In the meantime, I would like you to talk things over with Janus, to give you a broader perspective. In addition, we have brought along two other beings that you might like to interact with. Our ship Thelika, can communicate with you as Janus did. It can also facilitate a connection with Martha, another cyber-based intelligence aboard Thelika. I think you will find those discussions encouraging."

"Thank you, Sam. I am now in connection with those you have suggested and am feeling better."

That was quick, Sam thought. He was always amazed the way these cyber beings could connect with several sources at once.

"Sam, this is a complicated business, especially for Agar here and the Teratta," Carmen said. "I don't think that the complications we've uncovered affect the Agara or Agarians. I'd like to go the surface and be with the Teratta as I go over what we have learned."

"I'll go with you," Jesse said.

"Good idea," Sam said.

"I'd like to spend more time here, in a four-way conversation between Martha, Agar and Thelika." Travis said. "It would be good if one of us assessed what we have on the cyber-front."

"Sounds right," Sam said. "I'll be in touch with Janus. Ahleeto, I'm going back to Thelika. What are your plans?"

"I'll go back with you."

In the next moment, they all teleported away except Travis. On the surface, Carmen and Jesse returned to their place on the bench that had been provided. Carmen thought carefully about how to approach what could be a sensitive issue for the Teratta. She needn't have worried. It turned out that they had been listening in to the conversation below in the chamber. They had questions, but the topic was not new to them.

"So there is an intelligence in the chamber below called Agar, and the planet named Perillian by the Urritan is also sentient Carmen?"

"Yes."

"Are we communicating with both?"

"Yes. I believe that only the Teratta can communicate with, or sense feelings from Perillian. Agar cannot. I think the only being that the Agara and Agarians are communicating with is Agar in the chamber below. Your connection with the planet is one of the more wonderful aspects of life on the planet at this time."

"Why do you say that?"

"Your self-awareness occurred naturally. So did Perillian's, and I think the planet's self-awareness was a natural result of there being so many self-aware Teratta on its surface. Agar, Agara, and Agarians are very interesting, but you represent natural planetary development amid a carefully planned, unnatural setting."

"Thank you, Carmen. We appreciate your observation."

Carmen looked at Jesse, who smiled and nodded his agreement. They had talked about this before. The Teratta had been talking among themselves for a million years. It was time to expand their community.

"You're welcome," Carmen said. "Now I think it's time to introduce you to some new friends."

"Are they on the ship you traveled in?"

"One came with us, but not in the ship. Janus, could you introduce yourself to the Teratta?"

"Yes."

Janus introduced himself to the Teratta and described what he was.

"Janus, that is astounding. Carmen mentioned there would be more new friends. Are there more of you?"

"No," Janus said. *"Carmen?"*

"The other new friends I wanted you to meet are tree-like individuals somewhat like you," Carmen said. "They are called the Cheneshi. On their planet, they live below the surface of their oceans, rooted in the soil of the ocean bottom."

"Sways, could you introduce yourself to the Teratta?" Carmen asked. *"I'll bet that your two races have a lot to talk about."*

Part Two: The Rocara

13. Dominant Concerns

Planet Siana

Dahtra Selia, Satran of all Rocara, was in her quarters in the Septcium Tower in Tetara, the capital city of the Rocaran Domain. She looked in the mirror at the tiny, light-green scales that covered all Rocaran bodies. The scales were so small and so flat to the surface that they appeared as skin from the distance. They were as supple as skin, but the scales provided a much tougher epidermis.

Her scales were beginning to turn blue. She was aging in plain sight for everyone to see, but she was comfortable with that. Satrans were supposed to be aged and wise were they not? She checked that the short sleeves of her cream-colored blouse were not too short and allowed free movement of her arms. Her dark blue slacks fell to just above her sandals. Yes, she was ready to meet her public.

Dahtra was the youngest Satran, since Tablar Ken. He had forged the Rocaran Domain and created the vision of a unified and powerful Rocaran people one-hundred-seventy years ago. She was concerned that she might be the last Satran. The Domain was becoming unstable. She wasn't sure she could save it.

Enough about the future, she chided herself. There were other concerns to be dealt with today. Aluta, her assistant, had buzzed Dahtra's door twice now, a harbinger of some urgent matter that needed her attention. She was honored to have been chosen to be Satran five years ago by the Septcium, but she was happier when she was merely the Administrator of the Xartan Region. Again, enough! She had a Domain to hold together.

"Come in Aluta."

Aluta Seder had been her faithful and effective assistant since Dahtra ran the Xartan Region. When Aluta entered she looked as young and fit as when Dahtra had first hired her. The scales of her face and arms, where they showed outside her business attire, were still light green. Aluta was tall and slender as all Rocara were. She walked with the poise of a dancer.

The ear holes in the side of Aluta's head had a subtle decoration painted around them. It was the style now, though most of these decorations were much larger and brighter on others. Dahtra wasn't surprised that Aluta had chosen to make hers more subdued.

"Good morning Satran Selia."

Aluta could never bring herself to use the Satran's first name, even though Dahtra would have welcomed such familiarity. Since Dahtra life-mate Tomo had died two years ago, there was no one for her to be familiar with or confide in. Still, Dahtra knew it was better to maintain formality in private, lest there be a slip in public. Aluta's smile did warm the room, and that was enough.

"What do you have for me this morning, Aluta?"

"Production reports or I should say reports of declining production from the mines in the Materan Region. Administrator Solbe offered no explanation."

"Jerad Solbe, wouldn't, would he? The Administrator of the Materan Region seems to be happy with things as they are. He is not concerned if production goes down, so he doesn't think we should be. Put those on the desk in my office when you pass through there on your way out. What else?"

"Region Administrator Demis is in the City and would like to meet with you this morning."

"Did she say what was on her mind?"

"No."

Dahtra could tell from the crisp response of her assistant that Aluta had pressed Herata Demis for information and had been rebuffed. Dahtra smiled, understanding Aluta's reaction. Herata didn't mean to be aloof and rude. She was just simply more intelligent than any Rocara in Dahtra's experience and didn't explain herself to anyone. Even Dahtra had difficulty getting explanations.

Herata had one of the more challenging regions to administer, but in Dahtra's opinion she was doing a better job than any of her male Administrators, except Cartran Herc, who was now in charge of Dahtra's old region. Both Herata and Cartran were more advanced in their methods. The other three Administrators held to the old ways whether they worked or not, which was one element of Dahtra's concern for the Domain.

"Don't let Administrator Demis' manner bother you, Aluta. Herata is that way with everyone, including me. Set up a time we can both meet. If Herata has traveled this far to meet with me in person, she will have a very good reason."

Aluta didn't turn to leave. Dahtra waited.

"Aluta, is there more?"

"I wasn't sure I should pass this information along. I haven't been able to confirm it myself. It's more in the form of a rumor."

Dahtra knew Aluta would have found out what she could through her many sources before letting whatever it was even get on the list of possible discussion items. Dahtra also knew that she needed to know what it was, or Aluta wouldn't have brought it up.

"What does the rumor say?"

"It is said that Rulian Trace has found another planet in a star system on the border of the Tarkan Region. The planet is said to contain amazing deposits of needed minerals close to the surface, and that the surface is covered with very large trees which may be even more valuable than the minerals. The crew had an unusual excuse for not being able to land on the surface."

"Did the rumor also say whether the planet was inhabited?"

"Yes. Apparently it is sparsely populated by one primitive race which could be easily subjugated."

Dahtra knew that meant conquered and ruled. The Domain's economy was nearly totally dependent on the labor of the five sentient races that were from planets in star systems within the Regions of the Domain. Only Jerad Solbe's Terellan Region had no indigenous race, but laborers from the other regions were sent to his region to work in the mines.

Such reliance on the labor of Domain subject races was another reason that Dahtra was concerned about the stability of the Domain. It had worked for decades, but resistance among the subjects was increasing. The answer to this from the three administrators who held to the old ways was to increase the military budget and enact sterner measures to control the resistance. Dahtra knew that was a bankrupt strategy. Harsher measures would bring greater resistance.

"Any indication as to why the scout ship could not land?"

Again Aluta hesitated. Her assistant seemed to be having difficulty saying it.

"Aluta?"

"It was said that the crew was shaken by receiving a deep and threatening feeling that they were unwelcome and should leave the system."

"Just a feeling, no words of unwelcome?"

"Yes, Satran, just a feeling. It is said that Rulian, excuse me, Administrator Trace was furious when he stopped laughing at the ship's captain. He said he would travel there himself on the next trip to the planet. That trip has been delayed because of the upcoming meeting of the Septcium. Perhaps he will have more to say at the meeting."

"Yes, perhaps he will." Dahtra said, smiling. The five Regional Administrators, the Rocaran Military Administrator, Milan Chatrec, and the Satran were the members of the Septcium, which ruled over the Domain. A Satran was chosen by the other members to lead the Septcium. As with other Satran appointments, Dahtra was chosen because the other members felt she had the strength, wisdom and competency to wield the power of the office. She had the final word on all matters but was wise enough to listen. Administrators did not miss a meeting of the Septcium unless they were so ill that they were close to death. Too much was at stake.

"Thank you Aluta. I know there are more matters waiting for me at my desk, but I will remain here until the meeting with Administrator Demis."

"Yes, Satran."

Aluta left, closing the door quietly. Dahtra sat down in her favorite chair and looked out over Tetara's many crystal spires reaching so high as if to challenge the sky. Of course the one she was in, that of the Septcium, was among the tallest and was the grandest, but there were many variations, each new one built with the intent to outdo the others. These towers were both a tribute to the Rocaran sense of the aesthetic, and a demonstration of the wealth and prosperity of the Domain. In the mood she was in this morning the towers also seemed to be a statement of an arrogant race, and that arrogance was another element of concern for the Domain. Arrogant people made mistakes.

She sighed, sat back and thought about the potentially positive news of a new planet. It might supply much needed resources. Other sources within the Domain were beginning to show signs of decline, and the expense to expand them was prohibitive.

A case in point was the report now sitting on her desk showing lower production from the mines in the Terellan Region. Perhaps a more effective Administrator than Jarad Solbe could get more from the mines, but the mines were old, and it was likely that they already had given up their richest ore deposits. Increased resistance from the conscripts had also begun to hurt production in many locations.

There hadn't been a new star system added to the Domain for fifteen years. If this new planet was all it was touted to be, it would be a desperately needed addition. In her heart, she knew it would only stave off the ultimate decline in the Domain, but the time it gave them might be all they would need to make the necessary changes. Perhaps they could begin those changes by working with the indigenous race instead of conquering them.

She decided to go on the next trip to the planet along with Rulian Trace. He would not like it, but she would go anyway. She would assure him that he would still get credit for the find, and all the predicted riches would flow through his Region on their way to the Domain. If it was as great a find as has been rumored, it was appropriate that the Satran come and celebrate the valuable addition to the Domain.

She turned and looked around her luxurious quarters. The previous Satran's tastes had definitely been male oriented. She had brightened the place and made it more comfortable. When Tomo was alive, she spent more time with him living at their country estate. Since his death she hadn't been comfortable being alone in the place that was so full of pleasant memories.

She and Tomo had chosen to not have a clutch of offspring. They thought that they would not have the time to parent the typical two or three young ones given the challenges of their careers. Dahtra now thought that might have been a mistake.

Dahtra had grown up on Xarta and loved her early childhood which was spent in the rural areas. She preferred the country to the city. Her father had been the Administrator of the Xartan Region before her.

The only shroud over her childhood memories was the sadness in the eyes of the Xartan children who were on her father's estate. When she learned why, that the Xarta were subjects of the Domain, and that her father was the local ruler, she resolved to change things when she grew up. Then she became the local ruler and got lost in her career. Was her youthful resolve finally resurfacing? She knew that Cartran Herc felt as she did, though they had not discussed it openly. She wondered what Cartran was thinking about it now.

14. Hidden Agenda

Planet Xarta
Xartan Region Administrator Cartran Herc's office

Alone in his office, Administrator Cartran Herc knew he was planning his own demise. He had worked out several strategies for transitioning to self-rule on Xarta.

Cartran would have to involve others to take his plans any farther. He would need loyal Rocara to help, and he would have to engage the tribal leaders of the Xarta, beginning with Jemma Tolani.

He hoped she would agree to work with him. Jemma was the strongest and most respected leader among the Xartan tribes. Would she trust him after more than one hundred years of Rocaran Administrators ruling her people? He would have to start small. It would only be discussions at first, but any start would be dangerous.

Any leak of his activity would raise the ire of his fellow Regional Administrators. He would be ridiculed at the Septcium. He knew that Satran Selia felt as he did about the danger and injustice of ruling over the people who were native to the planets in the Domain, but she couldn't save him from the wrath of the other Administrators. The Regional Administrators, Rulian Trace, Jerad Solbe and Garan Ratra would definitely attack him the instant they heard of what he was doing. They would accuse him of aiding the resistance, and label him as a traitor to the Domain. He wasn't sure about

Administrator Herata Demis. She had never confided in him on anything.

Nor was he sure about Domain Military Administrator, Milan Chatrec. Chatrec's officers had to enforce discipline over the subjects of the Domain. Many officers had privately told Cartran they found such duty distasteful. He wondered if Chatrec felt that way. The other problem was that some of the military officers, while nominally reporting to Chatrec, were more loyal to the Administrator of the Region. It was so in his Region.

Dangerous? Yes. Career-ending? Likely. Life-ending? Possibly. He wouldn't be publicly executed for such a breach of policy, but his opponents might find a way to get rid of him. Raising the topic of ending Domain rule over planets that they had taken as their own, let alone talking it over with the subjects, was just too threatening to some of his fellow Administrators livelihood and their vision for the Domain.

All true, but he had to try. A society resting on the backs of resentful subjects was not a sustainable society. The Domain wouldn't last much longer with that as its foundation. There was already evidence that the resistance leaders had somehow developed a Domain-wide, multi-race network to coordinate their efforts.

So who could he trust? His aide Salus Donar? Cartran knew he could trust old Salus. They had often had candid discussions about the topic. Talking with him about taking action would put Salus in jeopardy. He would give Salus a choice. He called him to his office over the comm.

"Sir?" Donar asked, when he came into Cartran's office.

"Please sit down, old friend."

"Well, Sir, I will agree to 'friend,' but as to 'old'...."

"Point taken. I wanted to talk with you about something. I am about to step over a line. The actions I plan to take may be called traitorous and will set certain Domain leaders against me. I would like your help, but the path I'm about to embark on will put anyone who aids me in danger as well."

Salus stared at his boss without expression.

"Salus?"

"I know what it is you are about to do."

"You do?"

"Yes. Do you think anything you do escapes my attention? What kind of assistant would I be if I didn't keep myself aware of your work?"

"Well, what do you say?"

"I say what you are proposing is long overdue. You needn't have asked me if I would join your efforts to give this planet back to its people, but I appreciate that you gave me the opportunity to decline. Of course, I will join you. Be assured, I know how dangerous and sensitive this is. You can trust me. I think I know of others who can be trusted to join us, but let's wait until it is time. What's our next step?"

"I was planning to talk with Jemma Tolani," Cartran said.

"Good choice, but there are risks for her as well," Salus agreed. "She needs to maintain a healthy distance between herself and Rocaran leadership. If the resistance gets the idea she is cooperating with the Rocara against them, she will lose her credibility and possibly lose her life."

"How can we talk with her without getting her marginalized or killed?"

"There is no risk-free way," Salus said. "I should be able to arrange a connection between you and Tolani this afternoon. I know where she works, and I know the Rocaran who her boss is. And…Administrator Herc, thank you!"

Salus stood and left the room without saying another word. He apparently decided on his own that he needed to start work on the meeting right away. Cartran sat back in his chair feeling relieved that it had begun, and that his very competent and connected friend, Salus, supported him.

The Rocara did not abuse their subjects unnecessarily. If there was resistance when the Domain decided to take a planet as their own, they killed only the minimum number required to quell the resistance. There were no unnecessary beatings, or perversions. There was discipline and punishment for inappropriate actions of a subject, but only the minimum necessary to correct the behavior and get the person back to work.

Cartran thought that the most congenial relationship between Rocara and Domain subjects could be found on Xarta. Many Xarta held positions of responsibility within the Rocaran administration. It was common for a Rocaran and a Xartan subject to develop a casual friendship. Their respective positions always remained clear and that barrier would keep the friendship from becoming too deep. Still, it wasn't uncommon to see a Rocaran and Xarta subject sitting and enjoying a beverage together.

Jemma Tolani was a skilled fabric maker. She worked for a mill which made the fabric for both Rocaran and Xartan clothes. The fabric was prized throughout the Domain and was one of the few exports from the Xartan Region. Salus knew the Rocaran who owned the mill and knew his sympathies toward their cause. He gave the mill owner cover by saying that a visiting Rocaran mill owner wanted to have a casual word with Jemma about her work. It would be that afternoon, and Salus asked if Jemma could be allowed time to share a beverage with the visitor.

Salus brought a change of clothes to Cartran's office. It was a rainy but warm afternoon, so a hooded cape commonly used by the Rocara was included in the disguise. Dressed this way, with the hood over his head, Cartran was led by Salus out a back exit from the building and through the streets to a cafe. The establishment had a covered outdoor area in back. Salus had made sure there were no eavesdropping devices and no visual recording devices in the area. Jemma came into the cafe and walked to where they were seated.

Cartran watched her approach their table. She was tall for a Xartan, nearly as tall as a Rocaran. Her dark curly hair framed her light brown face. Like most Xarta, she was slender of build. She wore a simple tunic drawn together at the waist which covered plain linen pants that reached to her sandaled feet. Her brown eyes hinted of a sharp intellect. Cartran knew for a fact that the Xarta were intellectually equal to the Rocara, though no Rocaran would ever admit it. He knew if the effort he had in mind was to succeed, the best chance was with the Xarta.

Jemma had been told someone wanted to discuss fabric making with her. When she sat down and looked at the two Rocara sitting across from her, she only just managed to hold back a gasp, as she recognized Cartran Herc.

"Thank you for coming, Jemma, if I may use your first name," Cartran said.

"Given our relative positions," she said, "I assume you can call me anything you want."

"It is our relative positions I want to discuss with you," Cartran said. "I hope I can trust you to keep this discussion confidential."

"It would be my life if it were known I was talking with you. So yes, you can trust me. I won't tell anyone."

"We suspected that was the case, so we did what we could to reduce the risk for you. I have a matter of great importance to discuss with you," Cartran said.

Jemma continued to look at the Administrator without comment. Cartran thought that only the most direct statement would break down the obvious barrier between them.

"I want to transition to self-rule for subjects in the Domain. I want to start on Xarta. I want you to help me," Cartran said.

Jemma obviously hadn't expected that from the Regional Administrator. Her eyes remained on him but grew wider in disbelief.

"Just how do you intend to do that? If we walk away from the work that we do for you, the Domain will collapse under its own overfed weight."

"I need your help to create an approach that removes the burden of our government from your backs and keeps the Domain from collapsing. I don't see that the Xarta would walk away from work, though the conditions and compensation would have to change in your favor. We will need to establish a Xartan government. The interim officials would likely be drawn from the natural leaders among you."

"What about ownership? The mill I work in belonged to a Xartan years ago, before it was confiscated by the Rocara. There are many such cases. How does that factor into your vision for our future?"

"It will have to be worked out. Yes, your mill was formerly owned by a Xartan," Cartran said. "That was a long time ago, and the current Rocaran owner has made a substantial investment to refurbish it. For this to work there will have to be balance in everything we do. Although it might be difficult to accept it now, I would think the new Xarta may want to engage in trade with the Domain. For a trading relationship to develop, the steps taken during the transition would need to be agreeable to both parties. I know there will be deep resentment and a wish for revenge for all the years we have been ruling here. We will have to weather that as we move forward and keep it from destroying our chance for success.

"I'd say you need more than my help," Jemma said. "I'd also warn you, that you had better be ready for a fight and to persevere during what are going to be very difficult circumstances. If you are only half-hearted about this you probably will survive when it falls apart and you decide to walk away. Those you get to help you won't fare as well. So I ask you. Do you have that kind of deep commitment?"

Cartran looked Jemma in the eyes and felt her penetrating gaze.

"Yes."

She continued to look at him. What she saw apparently satisfied her.

"Good, because you will be sorely tested before this is over. You might not even live through your first meeting with those that you must win over to your cause. I won't be the one after your skin. I will help you, because I believe you are sincere, and that you have the power to make it happen. Others might kill you if they get the opportunity or abduct you to win some trivial concession. So be ready!"

15. They Will Explain

Planet Siana, Satran's Office, Septcium Tower

Satran Selia woke from her reverie when Aluta alerted her that it was time to meet with Administrator Herata Demis. She always enjoyed meeting with Herata. She was a bright, cheerful, active young Rocaran. It was challenge just to keep up with Herata's thinking when talking with her. This time there was something on her mind which brought her across the breadth of the Domain. Dahtra was eager to find out what it was.

Dahtra went through the door between her quarters and her office. She had just managed to sit at her desk when Herata breezed into her office trailed by Aluta, who had obviously tried to stop her so she could be properly announced. Dahtra saw the look of frustration on her assistance's face. She gave Aluta an understanding smile and signaled her to go back to her desk.

Herata appeared to be in a great hurry, for she chose to come to Dahtra without changing out of her traveling clothes. She seemed to only now realize it and took her cape off and laid it on a nearby chair.

"It's always good to see you my friend," Dahtra said. "Please try to take it easy on Aluta. She is only doing her job."

"Yes, yes, of course. I will apologize to her. I will work on my patience with others, if we survive what's coming."

Herata stopped and looked as though she was struggling with competing thoughts.

Dahtra had confidence that she sincerely believed something serious was happening. Dahtra rose from her desk and led them to a set of comfortable chairs that overlooked the city. Dahtra waited until they were both settled before engaging Herata again.

"What's coming?"

"What?" Herata asked.

"You said something is coming. What do you see?"

"Two things actually. One is important and urgent. The other is mysterious, extraordinary, and may be even more important."

"I've always found that it is a good idea to immediately address something that is both important and urgent. Let's start there."

Herata sat on the edge of her chair and looked at Dahtra with an intensity that caused the Satran to flinch a little.

"The Domain is resting on a knife's edge. We must take charge, and manage the change that is needed, or we will be thrust into years of conflict that will not end well for anyone."

So this *is* the time. Dahtra had a similar feeling, but she did not know when, and her thoughts did not possess Herata's certainty. Herata seemed to be speaking from an analysis that proved it to be true. Perhaps it would have been better if Herata had been chosen to be Satran in the times that were coming. No. She had skills that Herata lacked. They would work well together.

"I agree, although I have not worked it out as thoroughly as you have," Dahtra said.

Herata sat back, obviously shocked.

"You know! You know, and are doing nothing about it?"

"I need you to help me understand. But yes, I know we have to change. There are signs that ruling other people on their own planets is no longer working. Besides it is wrong. It has always been. There are indications that our subjects are about to revolt to demonstrate how wrong it is. As you say, that will not end well for anyone. Instituting the necessary changes will be opposed by powerful people. You know what Rulian Trace's solution for this will be."

"Yes, I do," Herata said. "That idiot will call for a stronger military to put down the resistance. Garan Ratra will agree with him."

"We can't let that happen. If we do, we will have two revolts on our hands."

"What do you mean?" Herata asked.

"I have said what we have doing is wrong for those we have subjugated, but it also doesn't suit us. We are not a people that are strongly driven to conquer others. Perhaps it was the vision Tablar Ken had needed to unite us one-hundred-seventy years ago, but it has never fit our psyche. We cannot tell the military to start enforcing stricter discipline, and perhaps murder people who only want what is rightfully theirs returned to them. To win the day we need to describe a viable future for the Domain."

"As I see that future, we will be a 'Domain' no longer!" Herata declared.

When Dahtra just stared at her without responding, Herata explained.

"Look at what we are, Dahtra. We are a people with ships that move things back and forth across the vast distances of our Domain. Some products are produced by us on planets where there is no indigenous race. Most products come from planets produced by the local people. None of our subjects has their own space fleet. They are dependent on products we move, and us to move them. The Rocara will turn into a race of merchants and shippers. We cannot call what we will have then a

'Domain.' We will be an association whose members depend upon each other for business and information exchange."

Herata had laid out quite a vision. Dahtra wished she had seen it first, because it was a good one. Dahtra could play her part by helping the Rocara and their former subjects make the transition. She thought that Herata and Cartran Herc would shape and mold things.

"Cartran!" Dahtra exclaimed. "Something has to be done quickly."

"What are you saying, Dahtra? What about Cartran?"

"Herata, are you willing to join me when I go public with this vision?"

"Yes!" She said without hesitation.

"Good, because we need to act right away."

"I agree, but why are you so concerned, and what does Cartran Herc have to do with it?" Herata asked.

"A long-time friend of mine, someone who worked on my father's estate on Xarta, has contacted me to tell me that Cartran has begun to make the changes we are talking about on his own. He has been talking to a Xartan leader about transitioning to self-rule.

"You and I cannot let his actions be condemned or him to be labeled a traitor. We do not want to lose one of our strongest supporters. We don't want what he has started, what we are talking about doing ourselves, to be condemned before we have a chance to make it legal. To establish self-rule as a legitimate goal I will introduce our new vision for the Rocara at tomorrow's Septcium."

Dahtra knew that what she had decided was as historically significant as what Tablar Ken had done when he formed the Rocaran Domain. Had he decided to do it one morning while talking with one of his staff? She did not know, but it had been that way for her. It seemed like a quick decision, but it had been building in her since she was young.

There were signs within that the Domain was becoming unstable. Herata arrived with her assessment and vision. Cartran had begun to move toward self-rule for the people of Xarta. Putting all this together Dahtra saw that it was time and made her decision.

"Good," Herata said. "Now let's talk about something really important."

Dahtra laughed. They had just decided to set the Rocara on a path to a dramatically new future. She wondered what could be more important than that. Apparently Herata thought something was.

"Remember Rulian talking about his subjects on Tarka, the Ortari?" Herata asked. "He described them as ignorant primitives that were not even smart enough to know that they had been conquered. That piqued my interest, so I went to Tarka and visited the Ortari on my way to the Capital. I spent a while living in their village with them and watching them interact with each other and with the Rocara.

Dahtra looked at Herata and wondered why this most intelligent Administrator chose to spend time in a primitive village. Perhaps it was time Dahtra set aside her judgments about those ruled by the Domain.

"What did you learn?" Dahtra asked.

"The Ortari are not ignorant, quite the opposite. They spoke little among themselves. It took time for me to understand that they did not need to talk. They are so deeply in the flow of the universe that they always act in concert with that flow, and do not need to discuss their actions."

Dahtra asked, "What does that mean? What is 'flow'?"

"I'm sorry. I've been studying what our philosophers have written about this. It is the term they use."

Philosophers? Dahtra wondered if her bright Administrator had drifted off into some esoteric philosophy, dulling the edge of her previously sharp intellect.

"Let me give you an example from what we have just been talking about." Herata said. "You have said that it is wrong for our people to rule over another people. The right action would be for us to interact with them on a co-equal basis. Ruling is inconsistent with the flow. Treating them as equals is aligned with it. It took us one-hundred-seventy years to come to that conclusion and although major, it is only one aspect of our lives.

"We take many actions every day. Some we feel good about, some we do not. The actions we feel good about are likely actions in alignment with the universal flow. Those that we do not feel right about are not in alignment. The Ortari are in nearly complete alignment with the flow.

"They don't act like a conquered people, because they are not. Rulian said they were indifferent to the Rocaran presence. I think he would find the truth even more insulting.

"When a Rocaran came to them and told them to do something, they would look at that Rocaran as if he were a child that needed attention. They would do what was requested, and then they would return to what they were doing before.

"After I had been with them a while, one of them who looked to be an elder in the village came up to me. It was the last day I could spend with them. I got the feeling the elder knew that."

"'What is it you seek daughter?' he asked. He spoke our language as if he had used it all his life. I told him I wanted to learn, to understand. He told me that I had come at a 'wonderful moment,' because 'something new was awakening.'

"I asked what he meant. He said that some of our people here have been 'touched by it.' I thought about the rumor that was circulating, about the way the crew of Rulian's scout ship was turned away from the planet they had discovered and asked him if that was it.

"He ignored my question. Instead he said that if I traveled there that I should not interfere. He said that there are 'others' there now, and that they 'will explain.'

"Then he turned and walked back to the group of Ortari he had left to talk with me."

"If it was the new planet he was referring to, how could the Ortari have known about it, or that there were others there now?" Dahtra asked.

"I can only guess that they sensed it, Dahtra, as a new thing in the flow. Think of the flow as a pond, and this new thing as a pebble dropped into it. My guess is that the Ortari have sensed the ripple caused by it. Maybe their awareness of the 'others' was also sensed in this way. I don't have an answer, but I believe there is something very special about the newly discovered planet, and that we should take care as we approach it."

Dahtra rapidly reassessed her thoughts about the new planet and the reason she was planning to go there. She originally thought her greatest challenge at the Septcium meeting was going to be to convince Administrator Trace to take a new approach to securing the planet. Now she might have to tell him that they would not be able to acquire it at all, and that would be after her declaration of her new vision for the Rocara.

After hearing Herata, the trip to the planet took on a whole new meaning. What was awakening? Who were the others they would find when they went there? What would they explain?

"I was planning to go to this new planet with Rulian right after the Septcium meeting. I now know that trip must occur immediately, before the meeting. You shall come with Rulian and me. I want you to be there when we encounter those who 'will explain' things to us. I'll have Aluta tell the others that the Septcium must be rescheduled. I'll also tell her to notify

Rulian that I am bringing my ship to pick him up on our way to this new planet. I agree. We need to know what is out there!"

16. An Unexpected Delay

Planet Tarka
Regional Administrator Rulian Trace's office

While Administrator Cartran Herc believed he was planning the end of his career, Administrator Rulian Trace felt that his career was on the rise.

Rulian was large for a Rocaran, both in height and weight. He wasn't fat. His extra weight went into his well-developed muscles. His skill in hand-to-hand combat was unequaled, though he didn't often get a chance to demonstrate his skill.

He towered over the Ortari subjects of the Domain who were pleasant, simple people, Humanoid in shape, and about five feet in height. Their naturally stout and strong bodies were covered by dark fur, including their small round head. The Ortari kept their placid demeanor, even when the much-larger Rulian attempted to intimidate them.

When the Rocara came to the planet Tarka they opened mines in a few locations on the planet. They told the Ortari that they were to work in the mines. They would be paid, but refusal was not an option. Some of the Ortari went to the mines, even the mines in the Terellan Region. Other Ortari went back to doing what they did before the Rocara arrived.

It was not surprising that the Ortari were not part of the Domain-wide network opposing Rocaran rule. They did not understand the concept of one person ruling over another. Such a thing was not possible in their reality.

The Ortari were an enigma to Rulian Trace and his subordinates. What kind of people could simply ignore the fact that they had been invaded and conquered? Resistance would have been easier to accept than the indifference the Ortari presented.

Herata Demis, had heard Trace talk about his Ortari subjects, and had recently asked him if she could come to Tarka and visit with them. It was fine with him if she didn't have anything more important to do than talk with a bunch of primitives.

She spent ten days in the Ortari community not far from the Rocaran buildings. He would have liked to have known what she was up to, but she came and went without spending any more time with Rulian than it took to say 'hello' and 'goodbye.' He thought it odd, but everything she did was odd.

Ortari behavior was only a minor irritant to Rulian. They worked the mines. Beyond that he didn't care. He was destined to be the next Satran and was working hard toward that end. He knew it would be a few years, but in the not-too-distant future he would be leaving Tarka, to live in the Satran's quarters on Tetara. During his long career he had always done things that added to his prestige, his wealth and the wealth of the Domain by demonstrating his competence and his commitment to the Domain.

He was taken aback when the other Administrators had selected Dahtra Selia as the Satran five years ago. He went along with it, biding his time until he would be selected to follow her. As one more step in that direction, he was in his office preparing a report that he would deliver at the upcoming meeting of the Septcium.

Rulian had made sure that word had leaked out about his scout ship finding a planet that would be a valuable addition to the Domain's resources. He knew the other Administrators would be envious. It had been years since a new, rich planet had been discovered.

Rulian knew the statistics of every planet in the Domain. The easily mined deposits of minerals on the new planet exceeded those on any other in the Domain. It had large deposits of valuable and rare minerals, which were found only in trace amounts elsewhere. The information he had given out only said the planet was a promising find.

Of course the other information about the curious feeling his crew had experienced had also leaked out. It was unusual, but it was nothing that would stand in his way. He would not let that oddity take the shine off his discovery of a new planet. He would make a commanding presentation which would reduce the strange event to a footnote. At least, that was his plan.

He finished the report and prepared to leave for Tetara. The Rocaran faster-than-light technology which traveled through null-space worked well, but it wasn't instantaneous. He would have just enough time to get there ahead of the meeting of the Septcium. He rose to leave his office, when his assistant, Kemel Bosin, rushed in.

"Sir, the Septcium has been rescheduled!"

Rulian couldn't believe it. The Septcium was rarely rescheduled, and it was usually because of some emergency. What had caused it this time? Wait. Herata Demis said she was going to the capital when she left. Did her appearance there result in this change? Maybe, but still, why? Was it somehow connected to her visit with the Ortari? That seemed unlikely.

He received his answer a moment later when his personal comm buzzed. It was the Satran's assistant. Rulian was surprised by the message. The Satran was coming to pick him up, and they were going to the new planet!

Part Three: Confluence

17. East Meets West

Aboard the Satran's ship, the Lacernia

It took two ship-days in null-space to reach Tarka, the principal planet of the Tarkan Region. During their time aboard Dahtra and Herata mostly stayed by themselves working on business from their respective cabins. During meals Dahtra asked Herata to explain more about the philosophies she was studying. Dahtra was beginning to develop an appreciation for Herata's perspective on existence by the time they were in orbit.

They did not go to the surface themselves. Instead they sent a shuttle down to bring Rulian Trace and a few of his scout ship crew aboard. After he and his crew were settled into their quarters Rulian was summoned to the Satran's cabin. He had not expected to find Herata Demis there as well as the Satran.

"Good day, Satran Selia, and you, Administrator Demis."

"Good day to you, Rulian."

Herata gave a brief nod.

"When you contacted me you only said that you were coming, not why, or that Administrator Demis would be with you."

"Yes. I thought it was better to be brief. I knew we would have time to discuss matters on the way to this new planet of yours. You have given the coordinates to my Captain, I assume."

"Yes."

"Good."

Dahtra took a moment to tell the Captain to get under way.

Rulian was never close to Dahtra so using her first name didn't work when he discussed matters with her. When she didn't offer an explanation, he had to ask.

"I am pleased that you have taken an interest in the planet we have found, Satran. I would have gladly explained the results of our survey at the Septcium meeting to save you this trip."

"Thank you, Rulian. I have chosen to see the planet for myself. There are mysteries surrounding it that are not addressed in a planetary survey conducted by Rocaran instruments."

"Are you referring to the strange story my crew brought back with them? You are seeking answers to something that might not have occurred."

"The Ortari know that it did occur," Herata said. "They believe that what your crew found has a significance that is far greater than the results of your survey."

Rulian turned to Herata and laughed.

"You spend ten days in a hut talking with those...," Rulian paused taking into account that the Satran was focused on him and chose his words carefully, "...those natives and brought back a story to our Satran urging her to investigate what you thought they were telling you? You of all people, Herata, with all of your intelligence and your rational mind, I would have thought you had better sense."

He stopped there realizing that he had just accused the Satran of being easily led on a fool's errand.

"It is just those qualities that Herata possesses that caused me to lend credence to what she told me, Rulian," Dahtra said. "If there is something unusual occurring at the edge of the

Domain, I think it is important enough that I should see what it is before we do anything else."

"Important enough to delay the meeting of the Septcium?"

"Obviously, or I wouldn't have delayed the meeting."

Rulian shook his head. He had the feeling that the treasure he had found might be slipping from his grasp. He didn't like that feeling.

"Can you tell me what you have told the Satran, Herata? I would appreciate some information about why this trip is so important."

"I will Rulian, but I doubt you will credit it the way the Satran has."

Herata told him of her experience with the Ortari, leaving out what the Ortari said about others being at the site. She and Dahtra agreed to keep that to themselves until they arrived. She attempted to help Rulian see what was behind the apparent indifference the Ortari were showing toward the Rocara. She was right. He didn't understand. He couldn't conceive of something so far from the reality he had created for himself.

"If there is nothing else, Satran, I'll go to my quarters," Rulian said sharply.

"How long do you think it will take for us to reach the system?" Dahtra asked.

"Nearly four days, Satran. I'll be working with my crew on exploration plans for the planet. I am at your disposal of course."

"Thank you, Rulian. Please don't worry. Once we shed light on this mystery, we will know how to proceed with the planet that you and your crew have discovered."

He nodded and left the room. Dahtra knew there would be no sense in discussing the reason for this trip with him again, so she would let him do his planning. She and Herata fell into the same pattern they had followed on the first leg of the journey.

They emerged from the four-day trip in null-space less than a ship-day from the target planet. Dahtra complemented the Captain on such precise navigation when he requested that she come to the Bridge. Herata had accompanied her. When the Lacernia shifted to in-system engines Rulian knew they were close and made his way to the Bridge. So all three leaders were there when the Captain made his announcement.

"There is a ship of unknown origin in orbit around the planet."

Dahtra and Herata had the same reaction to the announcement. Herata voiced it for both of them.

"The 'others,'" Herata whispered.

Rulian looked at her wondering what that meant. His reaction was quite different from theirs. He was worried that those on the other ship were there to claim his planet for their own.

They were on the Satran's ship, so he had to restrain his aggressive feelings. If he were on a ship of his own, he would have ordered the crew to make the weapons ready, and to increase speed toward the offending vessel. Instead he had to stand by and watch the Satran wonder what to do next.

* * *

On Thelika, Sam and his companions were readying themselves for what might come. They had been told by Josh that the new arrival was a different ship but contained the same kind of minds that had come before. Sam put Thelika and Martha to work as soon as the ship appeared, to glean what they could by listening in to the arrivals conversations and connecting to the ship's intelligence. They had a reasonable translation algorithm ready by the time it seemed appropriate to contact the new arrivals. Sam hoped the newcomers hadn't noticed the probes into their ship.

"We're being hailed, Satran," the Captain said.

"Put it on the main screen, Captain, and stand aside," Dahtra ordered. "Normally I would have you address the others. I wish to be the spokesperson this time."

On the screen a being that looked remarkably like a Xartan, except that this being had a light complexion and short light-colored hair. In all other ways, his features were very much like those of the Xarta.

"Greetings, I am Sam Baxter. We are called Humans."

"He speaks our language," one of the crew whispered.

With a sharp look from the Satran, the crew member and everyone else on the Bridge knew to keep quiet.

"Greetings, Sam Baxter. I am Dahtra Selia, Satran of the Rocara. You speak our language very well."

"I don't at present have a large Rocaran vocabulary, but our translator is working to increase it as we converse. Welcome to Perillian."

"Is this your planet?"

"No. Perillian is its own planet."

"How did it come by its name?"

"I would like to talk with you about that. The discussion would flow much better if we were to converse in person. We are still quite a distance from each other. I would be glad to come to your ship, along with one of my friends. Our shuttle will cover the distance very rapidly. I would also welcome you aboard our ship, Thelika, if you would prefer. Either way, I look forward to discussing a very interesting planet with you. If you need time to decide, Satran, we can wait."

"I would like a short time to discuss this with my colleagues, thank you. I will be back with you in a moment."

The screen blanked. Dahtra turned to Herata and Rulian.

"What is this?" Rulian demanded. "Who are these interlopers to set the rules for engagement?"

"Rulian, we are not 'engaging' them in the sense you mean. We are deciding where to have our first conversation with a race that seems to have advanced technology, and that may have very interesting things to tell us. No one at this point is an 'interloper.' I want to visit their ship at some point, but I would be more comfortable to have the initial conversation here. What do you two think?"

Herata thought it was a good way to start. Rulian, after relaxing his aggressive stance, said he would like to see if the shuttle Sam Baxter had discussed lived up to his claim.

Dahtra had the Captain connect the two ships again.

"Sam Baxter?"

"Yes. Please just call me Sam, Satran. We would be more comfortable using our first names."

"That is agreeable, and you can call me Dahtra. We would like to invite you to our ship. How many will be coming?"

"There will be two of us, myself and my colleague, Carmen Willathorpe. She goes by Carmen. Do you have a shuttle bay that can be pressurized, or should we bring pressurized suits?"

"It can be pressurized, but what air are you comfortable breathing?"

Sam had Thelika present the gas constituents, in atomic number format on the screen.

"These are the gasses in our atmosphere. We can tolerate minor differences in content. Are you able to decipher the gasses in this format?"

Dahtra looked to the Captain, who looked to his science officer, who took a moment to translate the information and then nodded. The science officer had their comm portray the gas content of the air inside the Lacernia in the same format.

"They look similar to me," Dahtra said. "Will you be comfortable breathing our air?"

"Yes. Please open the shuttle bay doors. We will be there shortly. In case you are concerned, we will not be carrying weapons of any kind."

Dahtra signaled the comm officer to end the call, and then looked at the Captain. He took that to be his cue to open the doors.

"Well, this promises to be an interesting ship-day," Dahtra said. "Captain, will you lead us to where we can greet our visitors when they arrive?"

"Yes, Satran. Will you need an armed guard?"

"Not with the greeting party, Captain. Please have a small armed party close by if we need them, but out of sight. I think we should take our visitors at their word, but not be foolish about it."

They hadn't left the Bridge yet when the shuttle appeared outside the shuttle bay.

"How could they possibly have arrived so quickly?" Rulian asked.

"They might have used a micro-shift through null-space," the Captain offered. "If so, they have more skill and perhaps more advanced technology than we do. It would have been very dangerous for us to attempt such a move within the star system."

The shuttle eased itself into the opening. The Rocara had just barely enough time to get to the door of the shuttle bay before the bay was completely pressurized. They opened the door and stepped out onto the platform next to the strange looking shuttle. It was made of shiny metal of some type, oval shaped, flat on the bottom, and had a large clear dome within which the two aliens sat. There appeared to be room for several more passengers.

Sam and Carmen weren't in a true space shuttle. It was a High-Speed Hover Probe, or HSHP, which maneuvered in the atmosphere using electric fans. It was airtight and had a supply of oxygen but could only be moved about in space by the occupants teleporting it. Before they left the HSHP Carmen turned to Sam.

"They are a beautiful people, Sam. They all appear to have a slender build and are about six feet tall. Those lovely, tiny green scales seem to cover their entire body. The round head which slightly protrudes at the front looks slightly lizard like. Their clothes make it impossible to see if there is a vestige of a tail."

"Thank you, Doctor Willathorpe," Sam said, smiling. "I don't think we should ask them about the tail."

Carmen nudged him gently with her shoulder. She wanted to sock him in his shoulder but didn't want to have to explain to their new acquaintances that they weren't fighting.

They retracted the dome and stepped out onto the platform. The two groups stood a short distance from each other, not sure how to proceed. The Rocara were dressed in what looked to be somewhat formal, colorful garments. Sam and Carmen had simple, light colored linen shirts and pants, and wore sandals on their feet. Dahtra stepped forward and bowed slightly from the waist. Sam and Carmen both bowed as well.

"Welcome, Sam and Carmen."

"Thank you, Satran," Sam said.

Sam and Carmen both had implants that translated the Rocaran words. The language was soft on the ears, and easy for the Human tongues to replicate when guided by the speaking-part of the implant.

"Let me introduce my colleagues. With me are Regional Administrators Herata Demis, and Rulian Trace. The Rocaran in the uniform is the Captain of the Lacernia, the ship we are in."

Each of the Rocara nodded when their name was said.

"Thank you for inviting us," Sam said.

"You are welcome. Let us move to more comfortable surroundings."

Dahtra let the Captain lead them out of the bay and into a room not far from the Bridge which had a large window. When they were settled in the room, the Captain returned to the Bridge to resume their travel toward Perillian. There was an oval table in the room which was arranged so that there was a view out of the window from all of the seats. The Rocaran anatomy was close enough to Human anatomy so that the seats around the table were a comfortable fit for Sam and Carmen. They looked out the window, but Thelika was too far away yet to be easily seen with the naked eye.

"Sam, you were going to tell us about the planet and how it was named," Dahtra said.

Sam had been thinking about how to start this conversation. There were many unbelievable things about the planet. They would talk about all of them with the Rocara if the conversation continued to be amiable. He had decided before hand to lead with the most important, unbelievable aspect of the planet.

"There are many things about the planet we should discuss, but the first thing you need to be aware of is that the planet itself is an emerging sentient. It feels and thinks but is only able to communicate feelings at this point. It was the planet that gave the crew of your first ship to arrive here the feeling that they were not welcome. It did not like what the crew was thinking about doing to it."

18. Proof and Consequences

It was interesting to Sam how being stunned could look different on each the faces of Rocara across the table. Dahtra and Herata were stunned, but their expression was one of understanding, as if his news linked with something they had thought about previously. Their eyes were wider than before and had a so-that's-it look to them.

The look on Rulian's face was more like disbelief mixed with frustration and anger. His eyes were also wide, but the lines around them seemed hard and stressed. Sam wasn't surprised when Rulian was the first to burst forth with his reaction.

"What's this? A planet that thinks and feels? Impossible!"

It was clear that Rulian was barely able to contain the feelings boiling up inside him.

"I do not believe you! For all I know it could have been you who tricked my crew into thinking those things!"

"Rulian!" Dahtra snapped. "Control yourself! These are our guests."

"I apologize to you Satran, but not to these...these peasants who are here for one reason, to steal this planet from us! Even if I believed you Sam Baxter, which I do not, what difference does it make? The Rocara would still occupy the planet and do what we wished with it."

"It is our belief, Administrator Trace," Sam said calmly, "that if there is a sentient lifeform on a planet, that planet belongs to them. It turns out that there are three sentient races on this planet in addition to the planet itself for a total of four. We are here to inform you of what we found, not to take the planet for ourselves."

All three Rocara stared at Sam in wonder. After a short time, Rulian continued his rant.

"It makes no difference! If we find something on the planet that we want, the Rocara will take it for ourselves! That is our way!"

Sam looked to the Satran.

"That has been our way, Sam," Dahtra said, sounding both saddened and embarrassed.

"That *is* our way, Satran," Rulian said. "Do not apologize. It is what has made us great."

"Things change, Rulian," Dahtra said.

"What are you saying? This is our way, Satran. This will not change!"

"This too might change, my friend," the Satran said.

It was obvious that Rulian was having trouble believing what he was hearing. It didn't stop him for long. He rose from his seat and gave the Satran a stern look.

"Take care, Satran of the Rocara! The old ways have served the Rocara for a very long time. The old ways also offer means to make sure that the leaders of our people do not take steps that are not in the best interest of the Rocara."

He turned and left the room. In the silence that followed, Carmen turned to Sam and looked into his eyes.

"Sam, are we okay here?"

"Yes, Carmen. We have friends to help us, but I don't think we need call upon them yet. I sense we have come at a time when there is a great difference in opinion regarding the future of the Rocara. Let's see how it goes. We may be able to help the Satran."

The Satran was obviously shaken. Herata Demis seemed angry. They looked at each other as if wondering what to do next.

"I apologize for Rulian's behavior. I would point out how trying recent circumstances have been for him, but nothing excuses his actions. I hope you are not so offended that you feel we cannot continue this discussion."

"His reaction was unfortunate, Satran, but we want to continue. There is so much you need to know."

"Good. If you will excuse me for a moment, I must see about Rulian. I don't know what he might do in such a state of mind."

She rose, went to the Bridge, and took the Captain aside.

"Captain, Administrator Trace is in a rage. I want you to send a security party, find him and confine him to his quarters. You are to post a guard outside his door to see that he does not leave. Tell his crew what has happened. I do not think we will have any trouble with them but watch them closely. Let me know when you have the Administrator in his quarters, and your assessment of his crew."

"Yes, Satran. What has happened?"

"Administrator Trace has directed threatening remarks at me, and at our guests."

"At you, the Satran of the Rocara?"

"Yes, but I do not want to make an issue of that right now. He does not appear to be in his right mind. We need to give him time to bring himself under control."

"Yes, Satran."

Dahtra returned to the meeting room and took her seat. She seemed uneasy but asked Sam to continue.

"I would like to ask a question first, if I may," Sam said.

Dahtra nodded.

"Administrator Trace spoke of 'the way of the Rocara.' Would you tell me what he meant?"

Dahtra sighed.

"The Rocaran Domain is made up of thirty-star systems over which we rule. In those systems there are five planets which have sentient races. We rule these races as subjects of the Domain. This has been our way for a long time, over one-hundred seventy of our years.

"There is evidence that the Domain cannot function in this way for much longer. I alluded to that a moment ago when I told Administrator Trace that we may need to change. I would rather not go into any greater detail as to what that change might be at this time. As you saw by Rulian's behavior, change won't be easily accepted by all Rocara."

"Yes, I see. Thank you. You and Administrator Demis have had a different reaction to my announcement about the planet's sentience. Could you tell me what was behind that difference?"

Dahtra looked at Herata and smiled.

"One of the races we rule is called the Ortari," Herata began. "They seem indifferent to our ruling them. A short time ago I spent time with them to learn the reason for this. I learned that they were neither oblivious, nor ignorant. Instead, they are very connected to the flow of the universe."

Herata stopped to look at Sam and Carmen to gauge their reaction to those terms. Seeing them both nod she continued.

"Near the end of my stay, an elder member of the community came to me and told me that something 'new' was waking, and that a Rocaran ship had visited it recently. When I asked him to explain, he said others were near the planet now, and that they would explain.

"I told the Satran about this, and she felt it important to personally investigate something so mysterious on the boarder of the Domain. She asked me to join her on this trip. Since it was Rulian's scout ship that was here before, it was appropriate that he be with us as well. As you have seen, he does not view these matters as Satran Selia, and I do. It is unfortunate, but true."

"Thank you for the explanation," Sam said. "I hope we can meet the Ortari at some time. They sound interesting. Though we have had a challenging beginning to our first meeting, I sense that you will be interested in what I have to tell you. What we have learned about the planet Perillian we could not believe ourselves until we were faced with the facts."

"You have said that there are four sentient races," Herata said. "Could you tell us about them?"

"Yes. I'll let Carmen describe them for you."

"The race that is most easily detected dwells in small villages around the globe on the three land masses," Carmen said. "They call themselves the Agara."

Carmen described the Agara and things they had learned about them.

"You said they were the most easily detected. Why is that?" Dahtra asked.

"From space they can be spotted with typical survey instruments. I imagine that the survey conducted by your scout ship recorded their existence. Another sentient race lives in the oceans. Even if they were detected, it would have been more difficult to see signs that would have led your scout crew to believe they are sentient. The third race lives on the land but gives no signs of sentience that would be detected from space. The land is covered by enormous tree-like beings. They are sentient and call themselves the Teratta. They predate the other two races by millions of years."

What Carmen had just described was so far from their experience that even the relatively open minded Dahtra and Herata were obviously having difficulty grasping it. Herata was the more scientific of the two.

"How did you determine the sentience of any of these races, especially the Teratta?"

"They spoke to us," Carmen said, "to our minds. I don't know if you have a word for mind-to-mind speech, but we call it telepathy. All three sentient races on Perillian are natural telepaths. The Agara spoke to us verbally, but they can connect with all other Agara across the planet telepathically."

Another pause. Sam had to admire the two Rocara. They were being hit with one new concept after another. Rather than rejecting them they took a moment and absorbed them.

"May we experience this phenomenon?" Dahtra asked. "Does one have to be a natural telepath to receive telepathic communication?"

Sam chose his words carefully. At this point he did not want to disclose that he and Carmen were both telepaths. He also wanted to hide teleportation from them as long as he could.

"I don't know if it will work for you or not. Perhaps the best way to find out is for you to come with us to the surface."

"Would we be welcomed?" Dahtra asked. "The Rocara who visited earlier were told to leave."

"They wanted to 'cut and dig and take things away' according to the Teratta's interpretation of what the planet felt your crew was here for. You don't seem to have those intentions. Also we've been accepted, and you will be with us."

Just then the door to the room opened. The Captain entered and waited by the door for the Satran to acknowledge him and beckon him into the room. He came over to her, leaned down and spoke softly.

"It has been done, Satran."

"And his crew members?"

"They understand our response."

"Thank you, Captain," Dahtra said out loud. "We are planning to leave with our visitors on their shuttle. I would like you to continue toward the planet and enter an orbit not far from their ship. Should I be concerned about things aboard during my absence?"

The Captain stood up, ramrod straight.

"No, Satran. You need not be concerned. The situation is firmly controlled. There will be no further disturbances, but your leaving unaccompanied causes me concern."

"Administrator Demis will be with me."

"I am sure that will be a comfort for you, Satran, but for me it just doubles my concern. Might it not be wise to take an armed party with you?"

"Thank you for your concern, Captain. Yes, I think that would usually be wise. In this case I think we will be safe. Still to put your mind at ease, I will take one armed member of your security team, if there is room in the shuttle."

Dahtra looked at Sam.

"I understand the Captain's concern. We will accommodate the addition of a guard."

The guard was chosen. The five of them made their way to the shuttle bay accompanied by the Captain. Once on the platform next to the HSHP, the Rocara looked uneasy about their upcoming journey. Sam offered a hand to Dahtra and helped her into the HSHP. Carmen did the same for Herata and the guard. The five seats were able to be rotated but were locked looking forward. Once they were seated, Dahtra turned to the Captain still on the platform.

"After the dome is closed, I'll give you the signal when it is safe to depressurize and open the bay to space."

When the dome was closed Dahtra looked at Sam and he nodded. She signaled the Captain. He left the bay, closed the door behind him and signaled the crew member to start the process of depressurizing the bay and opening it to space. When that was done, Sam chose a spot outside of the ship and teleported them to that spot. He looked around at the Rocara, registering their surprise.

"You will have to tell me more about how this shuttle can move so rapidly," Dahtra said.

"As we get to know each other better, Dahtra, we can both share more. For right now, please don't be alarmed, but in the next instant, we will be in a clearing on the surface of the planet."

Sam had chosen the clearing near the Teratta, Josh. They landed gently on the ground. Sam again looked around to make sure the Rocara were not too disturbed. As best as he could tell, from the Rocara expressions, they looked shocked, but had successfully accepted the proof of their eyes.

He opened the dome and was the first one out. He went around the small ship and opened the other door and helped the Rocara safely to the ground. Once he was sure they would not fall, he went over and put his hand on Josh.

"Hello, friend. I have brought some visitors from the race that visited in that earlier ship. Carmen and I have not disclosed that we are telepaths, but we have told them that you are. So we will be talking to you verbally. Also, we are not telling them about the artificial intelligence below the surface, or how long-lived you are. We think that is best at this point."

"I understand," Josh replied.

Sam turned to Dahtra and the other Rocara, still leaning with his hand on Josh.

"The Teratta didn't have individual names. This is the first one we communicated with. He allowed us to call him Josh to make conversation move more smoothly."

The Rocara nodded their heads, still not quite believing Sam.

"Josh, could you make a bench for our visitors. They have come a long way and may need to sit down for a moment as they try to absorb all of this."

"Certainly, Sam," Josh said to everyone telepathically. *"Welcome Satran Selia, Administrator Demis, and crew member Teran."*

The eyes of the Rocara opened as wide as Sam had ever seen them. They looked even more amazed when before them Josh shaped the lower part of his trunk into a bench large enough for all five of them to sit on. Josh created an alcove that curved inward into his trunk. It was about ten feet wide and tall and was curved at the back corners and top. The bench stretched between the two sides of the alcove. All the surfaces were covered with very smooth bark.

Again Sam admired the fortitude of the Satran, when Dahtra walked over and sat down on the bench.

"Thank you, Josh," Dahtra said. "Sam was right. After the events of today, sitting down was exactly what we needed. Thank you for accommodating us. Come join me, Herata, Teran. Sam, do you think we could have some water?"

Sam nodded. A few minutes after they were settled on the bench, Sela came into the clearing accompanied by two others from the village. They carried jugs of water and cups for the five visitors. After drinking the water Dahtra thanked Sela and the others. Sela nodded and spoke to them. Since Sela spoke in English, Sam had to translate.

"She said, 'You are welcome. Now you have a part of Agar inside you.'"

Dahtra looked concerned. "Does that mean that there is something in the water? What is 'Agar'?"

"We thought so when they told us that," Sam said. "We checked and haven't found anything in the water or ourselves. So I wouldn't worry. 'Agar' is their name for the planet."

"I see what you mean, Sam, about how this planet is not for others, but belongs to these people."

"Yes, when approached from the ground in this way, it is easier to understand, Dahtra. Would you like us to show you more of the planet?"

"No, Sam. Perhaps another time. I have a meeting of the Rocara leadership, which I must convene immediately. Administrator Trace will want to air his opinions and grievances to his peers. A Satran has never had to confine an Administrator as I have. There will be an accounting. There are other matters that will be even more controversial to discuss at the meeting. I cannot delay any longer."

"I understand," Sam said. "Perhaps another time, then."

Dahtra looked over to Herata as if seeking confirmation to an idea she had. Herata seemed to know what she intended and nodded her head. Dahtra turned back to Sam.

"Sam, this has been an extraordinary experience for us. Would you be willing to accompany me on our trip back to our Capital, and describe these wonders to the Septcium?"

Sam looked at Carmen.

"Suggestions?"

"If we can convince the Rocara to leave this planet alone, it will make the job of protecting it much easier. They are the only other race that knows about it."

"That makes sense to me, too, Carmen."

Dahtra watched as the two Humans seemed to stare at each other and wondered what passed between them. Sam turned to her.

"Yes, Satran. I would be honored to be allowed to speak with your leadership group. I have a suggestion as to how to go there."

"Yes?"

"If you are willing, we could put the Lacernia in the hold of our ship, Thelika. As you have seen, we are able to move our ships rapidly. We could get to your planet in the same time it took us to move from your ship to the surface of Perillian."

Sam saw the skeptical looks on the Rocara.

"Yes, it is hard to believe, but it is true. If you are in a hurry to have your meeting, we can get you there much sooner."

Dahtra looked to Herata.

"It will be interesting to find if this is true, Satran," Herata said.

That was enough for Dahtra. "We accept your offer, Sam."

19. Septcium

Sam and the others boarded the HSHP and went back to the Lacernia. When they were aboard the Rocaran ship, and the Captain learned what was to happen, he was skeptical, but followed the Satran's orders. He stopped the Lacernia were it was. Sam contacted Thelika and asked that she move to the Lacernia's new position.

Dahtra asked the Captain to accompany her to Rulian's quarters. They found Rulian working at the desk. He rose when they came in.

"Satran, Captain."

"Rulian, I am sorry to have had to confine you to your quarters. Are you more at ease, now?"

"I have myself under control, if that is what you mean, but you will have to answer to the Septcium for your actions, Satran."

"I realize that, Rulian. Confining you was not a small matter."

"Not only my confinement, Satran. There is the matter of your conduct with regard to the strangers and the new planet."

"I am ready to present my case, as I am sure you are. I will convene the Septcium as soon as we return. Will you need to stop at your home base before attending the Septcium meeting?"

"No Satran. I have everything I need. When will we be leaving?"

"That's another thing I wanted to tell you about."

When she had finished Rulian looked at her.

"I think it is unsafe to show these people with their unknown technology the position of our home world, Satran. As you have already decided, I will join you and see what can be seen."

The Lacernia was loaded into Thelika, and the coordinates for Siana were provided. Sam led the Rocara to Thelika's common room. There they met Travis and Jesse. The Rocara were given one more surprise when Ahleeto appeared and introduced herself and explained her appearance.

"So this is a Lorengi ship, then?" the Captain asked.

"Yes," Sam answered.

"Where is the crew? Where's the Bridge?"

"Thelika requires no crew," Ahleeto said. "She operates herself. There is no Bridge."

"That is amazing! Can you tell me more?"

Ahleeto looked at Sam who answered the question.

"As I said to the Satran, Captain, when we get to know each other better, we can share information with each other."

The Captain looked disappointed.

Sam directed their attention to the main screen in the common room.

"Below us you see Perillian," Sam said. "In a moment, Ahleeto will ask Thelika to take us to your planet, Siana. The image will change almost immediately, presenting a view of your home world. Are you ready?"

"Yes, we are," Dahtra said.

The image on the screen changed to show Siana. The Rocara, even Rulian, gasped.

"Is that really Siana?" Herata asked.

"Yes it is Administrator Demis," Thelika said. "It is midday in your capital city, Tetara. Satran, if you will speak, your image and voice will be communicated to your planet."

Dahtra did her best to conceal her astonishment that the ship was speaking to her, and addressed Siana ground control, letting them know she was inside the ship they could see, and that soon Lacernia would emerge from its hold.

"Sam, will you agree to be our guest in the Septcium Tower?" Dahtra asked. "It would be the most convenient way to be ready to address the Septcium meeting."

"What?" Rulian interrupted. "Satran, the Septcium is a private meeting for you and Administrators only."

"A private meeting to which we sometimes ask others to make presentations. I have asked Sam to tell us what he knows about the new planet."

Disgruntled, Rulian didn't agree, but did not protest. He apparently just added it to the list of offenses he would raise against the Satran.

Sam agreed to be the Satran's guest. He led them back to the Lacernia in Thelika's hold. The rest of the Thelika crew would remain aboard, in orbit above the city. Sam teleported the HSHP from the Lacernia to the landing pad at the Septcium Tower. After the HSHP left, the Rocaran Captain moved the Lacernia out of Thelika's hold.

When Sam arrived at the quarters the Satran had arranged for him in the Tower, he communicated to those aboard Thelika that he was alright. He looked out the window at the impressive array of architecture spread out before him. After consuming a light meal that had been delivered to his room, Sam focused on what he would say at the meeting of Rocaran leaders.

* * *

The Septcium met on the same floor of the tower as the Satran's quarters. The meeting was to start later that day so the other Septcium members would have time to get to the meeting. As she paced slowly in her quarters, Dahtra wished it would have been set for an earlier time. She was nervous.

Dahtra knew that she had two strong supporters in Herata and Cartran, and that she had the strength to wield the power of the office she held. She also knew that she held the office only as long as the Administrators thought it was in the best interest of the Domain.

It wasn't that Satrans were replaced every time they took a position that the Administrators did not like. It would be a meaningless office if that were the case. In fact there was only one instance since Tablar Ken's time that a Satran had been 'retired' early.

Her new vision for the Rocara might not only get her removed from her position, but it might also split the Septcium and the Rocara—create a wound so deep that it could not be healed. She could live with being deposed, but she would be deeply saddened if her action destroyed the Domain instead of making it stronger.

Apparently she had paced away the time. Dahtra was surprised when Aluta alerted her that the Administrators had assembled, and that it was time to begin the meeting.

She walked from her quarters to the Septcium private meeting room. There was another room where the Septcium held public sessions, but this was the room where all serious matters were decided. The heavy doors that were at the Satran's private entrance opened as she approached. She walked into the room, erect, with her chin up. She acknowledged the Administrators and took her seat at the head of the oval table.

It was the original Septcium table. It was moved to its present location twenty years ago when the Septcium was moved into this new tower. It was a thick table, made from an exotic wood only found in one place on Siana. Its solidity was symbolic of the strength of the Domain and the Septcium which guided it. The room was brightly lit by the sun shining through crystal windows which were all around the room.

Strength with a bright future would be an apt description of the thought that went into the room's design.

Dahtra looked around at the Administrators, assessing them. Milan Chatrec was on her left. The aged Military Administrator smiled at her. They had known each other since she was young, living on her father's estate. How would Milan react to her new vision? She thought he would embrace it.

Then there was Jarad Solbe. Her proposal might affect him less than the others, as long as a way was found to keep his mines in operation. If she was successful this morning, she would seek a replacement to lead the Terellan Region. Jarad had essentially retired already. It was time to make it official.

Next to Jarad was Garan Ratra, Administrator for the Materan Region. Garan and Dahtra had never been close, and she found it difficult to read him. He ran his Region effectively, but resistance was almost as strong there as it was in Cartran Herc's Xartan region. Would he balk at what he would see as "giving in" to the resistance? Or would he see the wisdom in the new path for the Rocara?

So on one side of the table she had one likely supporter, one likely indifferent, soon-to-be-retired, and one potentially strongly opposed. On the other side was Rulian Trace, Herata Demis, and Cartran Herc. She knew Herata and Cartran would support her proposition. That left Rulian.

The Region Rulian Trace administered also had two planets with sentients. According to Herata, the Ortari were not part of the resistance because they saw nothing to resist. That thought brought a smile to her face which she quickly disguised by rubbing the scales just above her mouth.

According to reports that had reached Dahtra, the other race in Rulian's region was active in the resistance. She knew that Rulian would be against her vision for the Rocara and propose stronger sanctions against the subjects who were opposing the Rocaran rule.

He wanted to be the next Satran over a Domain that enforced his rule. He was building his wealth and wouldn't want that process interrupted. He would object to her proposal and would be furious when he found that he wouldn't get control over what he thought of as an extremely valuable new planet. He would use recent events at the planet Perillian to support his position that the Satran was leading them in the wrong direction.

The Administrators were getting restless as she surveyed the players in today's drama. It was time.

"Thank you my friends for being patient while I gathered my thoughts. We have important things to discuss today. I'm sure each of you has something you want to bring to the table today, but I must ask you to set them aside for now. Recently I went with Administrators Trace and Demis to visit the planet that one of Rulian's scout ships had discovered. The results of the survey conducted by the crew of the scout ship were exciting. What we found when we arrived was even more amazing.

"We met members of two other races that were visiting the planet at that time. They had been researching the planet and found not one but several sentient races on it. I have asked the head researcher from that group to address us today to describe what he found. His name is Sam Baxter. I will ask my assistant to bring him in."

She had given Sam guidance when describing the meeting he would be entering, but she did not know what he would say when he arrived.

Sam came into the room, took in how its formal setting and table contrasted with the daylight which brightened the entire room. He went to the end of the table opposite to where the Satran sat. All of the Rocara looked up at him and his casual dress, as if wondering what the Satran was thinking bringing such a shabbily dressed individual in to address them.

141

When he spoke in a solid clear voice using their native language they were forced to revise their judgment of the visitor. He told them about the planet Perillian and those who lived on it. What he told them lent more understanding to the Satran's actions. He finished and awaited questions. There were none.

"Thank you, Sam. Would you please wait for me in my office?"

When Sam had left the room, Dahtra surveyed the table again. She needed Rulian and Garan to support what she was about to propose. Jarad was replaceable, but the other two had followers among the Rocara, who would be influenced by their actions and words. She knew she had already lost Rulian's support, she wasn't sure about Garan.

"I have asked you to set aside what you have brought to the meeting today. Perhaps you will see why I have asked for this time when you hear what I have to say. Rulian, I know you have a grievance you wish addressed at today's meeting. I ask you to hold that until the end."

It was obvious Rulian wasn't happy about it, but decorum required that he acquiesce.

"We Rocara are a strong people and have lived in a time of prosperity and abundance for many, many years. We have prospered in part at the expense of those we rule. When we found resources on their planets that the Domain needed we took the planets for our own and subjugated the residents to our rule. This was the vision Tablar Ken gave us. We have been successful, but it is time for a change.

"We have seen that our subjects have begun to oppose our rule. It has begun slowly, and for the most part been non-violent, so far. If I felt we were in the right, I would act to suppress their actions, but we are not.

"The Rocara themselves grow dissatisfied with the role we have cast ourselves in, as conquerors and rulers. There is growing sentiment that we need to change. Most will not speak openly of their dissatisfaction. I hope that is because they respect their Septcium leaders rather than that they are afraid of reprisal. So we of the Septcium must speak and act for them to bring about the needed change.

"I declare today that the Rocara Domain will move in the direction of self-rule for our former subjects. If we can be called a 'Domain' in the future, it will be a Domain containing only star systems that do not have sentients on any of its planets.

"This is a dramatic change and will have to be handled carefully. Our subjects may feel it is a time for reprisal against their overlords. Some might wish for us to immediately leave their planets. Perhaps we should be ready to do that if their demands become strident enough.

"I think that our subjects will come to understand that the transition would be best served by us supporting them while they build their own system of self-rule and administration. We can help keep the wheels on the cart while they are getting their new governments established.

"What I hope we will become to them is a valued trade partner. We have the fleet to support the interstellar trade they have become dependent upon. Those that want to may develop their own space fleet, but that will take time. The needed knowledge and infrastructure are both owned by us.

"This is my vision for the Rocara and those we have ruled in the past. I value each of you at this table and will need your support as we implement this vision."

She stopped. She had looked around the table as she spoke, noting but not being affected by the reactions she saw. Herata was smiling. Cartran appeared to be pleased. Jarad was dull as ever. Milan smiled quietly. Garan and Rulian had the same solid stone expressions of barely controlled anger. She had the votes, but this wasn't a voting matter. The Satran had spoken. The direction had been set. She would consider advice on how to implement it, but it would be done.

"It looks like you have something to say, Rulian. Please let us hear it."

"Satran, you will destroy the Domain if you go ahead with this!"

"Rulian, as I have declared, this will be implemented. I agree that the Domain as we know it today will be changed. It needs to change. The Rocara are strong and will weather the changes. They will have the burden of being overlords lifted from their shoulders and be happier because of it."

"We should deploy more military, and beat down the subjects who oppose us," Garan said.

"The military will not take on the role of disciplining or killing those who oppose us," Milan said. "They will support the Satran. They are tired of being our enforcers. Yes, even those you think support you instead of me will come around. I know those officers better than you do. Do not count on the special privileges and rewards you have been giving them to make them break from the Satran. They are Rocara first. They will not defy her. They will know what Satran Selia declares is right for the Rocara."

"I know this will be difficult," Dahtra said. "I hope you will find it easier to support me as time goes on, but make no mistake, I will have your support!"

Looking at the others she made it clear that their support was a requirement of their remaining in their posts.

Dahtra rose, signaling the end of the Septcium meeting.

"With your indulgence, Satran," said Rulian, "I have a matter that must be discussed. I assure you it will not take long."

Dahtra sat back down and signaled for him to proceed. Rulian described the events at Perillian from his point of view and told them of his confinement. He didn't dwell on any of it. Instead he rose out of his chair and stared at Dahtra.

"I have respected the leadership of our Satran in the past, but because of her recent actions and the proposed change for the Rocara that she has announced today I declare that she is unfit for her position. I know that I do not have enough support at this table to have her removed from office by a vote of the Septcium. Therefore I claim the ancient right of Tezaxt. She must fight me and win to keep her place!"

20. Tezaxt

Planet Siana, Tetara, Septcium Meeting Room

Rulian remained standing, waiting for an answer to his challenge. The rest of the Administrators were shocked into silence.

Dahtra's shoulders sagged. It wasn't the prospect of death that had her in its grip. It was a deep disappointment. *Have we come no further than this in the nearly two-hundred years since the Septcium was established? Would this one Rocaran throw us back into the inter-tribal conflict that drove Tablar Ken to form a unified Rocaran people—one tribe, one leadership.* No matter what choice she made, she was concerned this would not turn out well for her people.

"What from-the-swamp is a Tezaxt?" Cartran Herc asked.

"It is an ancient method that was available to challenge a tribal leader who someone thought wasn't doing what was needed," Milan Chatrec said. "It also has been a method used by some ambitious Rocara to promote themselves into the leadership position."

"It's barbaric," Herata said. "Surely it can no longer be called into use."

"Unfortunately it can," Milan said. "It was one of the things that Tablar Ken was trying to eliminate. The Rocara were losing many excellent leaders to local, reckless Rocara who wanted to have the position, but didn't have the leadership skills to attain it. Tablar negligently did not take Tezaxt off the books. So it is still available in Rocaran law, though no civilized Rocaran would use it."

"The Satran is no match for Rulian," Cartran said. "Surely this kind of mismatch has happened in the past."

"Yes, it has," Milan said. "When the one challenged is so out matched, they have the right to appoint a champion who is more closely matched to the challenger."

"Then choose me as your champion, Satran," Cartran said. "I am not afraid to fight this bully."

"Take care, young master Herc," Milan said. "You have not heard the rest. This is not a sporting event. This is a tooth-and-claw fight to the death. Only one walks away from this fight, and he who wins takes with him everything that the loser owned—everything. I'm sure that Administrator Trace has that very thing in mind, don't you Rulian?"

Rulian didn't answer. He kept his eyes on Dahtra, expecting an answer.

As Satran, Dahtra knew that she had the ability to dismiss the challenge and remove Trace from his position of Administrator. She also knew her people. They were civilized, but not so civilized that they wouldn't attach a taint of dishonor to one who used her position to avoid a fight, even if it were one she couldn't win.

She rose from her chair. She looked at the members of the Septcium. Herata, Cartran, and Milan were sympathetic, understanding her difficult position. Jarad Solbe was indifferent. Garan Ratra was smiling. Then she looked at Rulian.

"I accept your challenge, Regional Administrator Trace. As has been discussed, being so outmatched, I will have to appoint a champion."

She turned to Cartran.

"Not you my young friend. I don't doubt your valor, or your ability. You are far too valuable to the Rocara to be risked in the farce that Administrator Trace has proposed.

She looked back at Rulian.

"As for you, and your challenge, Rulian, I shall appoint my champion this afternoon. You will not know who it is until the time of the combat. The challenge will be met in the performance arena tomorrow morning at an hour that I will announce when I tell the Rocara everything that has happened here today. I hope you realize the danger you have put our people in, Rulian.

"Milan, please join me in my office."

She turned and left through the Satran's doors.

The other members of the Septcium rose. Cartran, Herata, looked at Rulian in disgust and left. Jarad ambled out as if nothing happened. Milan turned to Rulian as he was leaving to join the Satran.

"You are a danger to the people, Trace, and a coward."

"When I am Satran old one, you will be gone."

"No one will serve you willingly. Think about that as you plan your future."

Milan left. Garan came over to Rulian and slapped him on the back.

"Bold move. Hope you win," Garan said, and then left the room.

Rulian looked around the room and wondered what his blind ambition had gotten him into. A fight to the death. He hadn't killed anyone in his entire career, well no Rocara anyway, just a few subjects. Now he would have to kill one of his own. What would the people think of a new Satran who came to the office with Rocaran blood on his claws?

* * *

Dahtra walked through the outer office on the way to her own and noticed Sam sitting there. He has come at a tragic time in her people's history. Then she played that thought over again in her mind. *He has come at this time. Why is he here of all times? Maybe there's a reason.*

"Sam will you come into my office? Aluta, send Administrator Chatrec in when he arrives."

Dahtra had just sat behind her desk, and motioned Sam to one of the chairs in front of it when Milan came in. He looked askance at Sam and then at Dahtra.

"Will we be talking about this in front of your guest?"

"Yes, Milan. Please close the door and sit down."

She explained to Sam what had happened.

"Are there weapons involved?" Sam asked.

"No," Milan said. "This is tooth-and-claw combat. No aids of any kind may be used. Anyone trying to do so is shamed, disqualified and loses everything as if he had died in the fight."

"Milan, you seemed to have studied this," Dahtra said. "Are there rules as to who the champion can be?"

"No restrictions. Any sentient being willing to risk their life is eligible. What are you thinking, Satran?" Milan asked, concerned where this might be going.

"Nothing. I'm just making sure I know what my options are."

"I've seen Administrator Trace," Sam said. "He seems larger in the chest and shoulders than any other Rocaran I have seen."

"He is, Sam," Milan said. "He is skilled in claw-to-claw combat, better than anyone he has come up against."

"What will you do, Dahtra?" Sam asked. "Do you know of anyone as skilled as Trace?"

"No, I do not. I would take the fight myself, but I am sure I would lose. I'm not afraid of my death. I am afraid for my people under Rulian's leadership."

Sam thought about the importance of this to the future of the Rocara. Dahtra was right. He would volunteer himself, but he didn't want to kill anyone. Then he had an idea.

"May an opponent yield, give up the fight before being killed?" Sam asked.

"Yes," Milan said, "though few of these combats have ended that way. There is a taint of cowardice associated with such an ending."

"Good. Then choose me as your champion. I don't want to kill Trace, but I believe I will be able to wear him down until he can't get up, and he will yield."

Both Rocara looked at Sam in disbelief. Milan spoke for both of them.

"Sam, you are not qualified."

"You just told the Satran that any sentient being would do. I am one."

"That's not what I meant. Let me show you."

Milan reached out his hand, stretching it until sharp claws appeared at the end of each of his five fingers. Then he opened his mouth. The jaw adjusted so that it could be opened wider than seemed possible from the look of a Rocaran with his mouth closed. This was something Sam hadn't seen any Rocaran do since he met them. Milan showed Sam a mouth full of sharp, carnivore teeth. Milan then slipped off his boot and demonstrated that there were claws at the end of the three toes on his foot.

"Well, I just won't let him touch me then," Sam said, laughing.

"I can't let you do this Sam," Dahtra said sadly. She knew she didn't have another champion, but Sam would die in the combat sooner than she would.

Before either of them could speak another word, Sam leapt from his chair, stood behind Milan and held him in a chokehold. It was done so quickly that neither Dahtra nor

Milan had followed the progress. Sam stepped away just as quickly and sat back down.

"I hope I didn't hurt you, Administrator Chatrec. That is not a move I would use on Trace, because with his claws he would shred my arms before he expired. I did it just to show you that I am fast enough to avoid being struck by Rulian. Besides speed, I have a form of combat that Rulian has never heard of and won't be able to defeat."

"What do you think, Milan?" Dahtra asked.

"It's your challenge, Satran. I think Sam may be right. I have never seen anyone move that fast. If he has defensive skills to go with that speed, I think he might be able to do what he says he can."

"Alright, Sam. I reluctantly accept you as my champion."

"Since you are the one who is challenged, Satran, I assume you won't be managing the event. Who will you appoint to be what we would call referee?" Sam asked.

Dahtra looked at Milan.

"Will you do that for me, Milan?"

"Of course, Satran."

"Thank you."

"I will need a short time to do what we call 'limbering up,'" Sam said. "It would be best if I could do it just before the bout began. Can that be arranged?"

"I will hold the beginning until you have finished, Sam," Milan said.

Milan left to plan for the event that would take place the next day at the Performance Arena, located across the avenue from the Septcium Tower. Inside was a large circular performance area one hundred feet in diameter, with seats rising up all around the sides. Traditional dance exhibitions, plays, and music performances were held there. Sometimes it was used for the Rocara form of professional wrestling. There had never been a Tezaxt held there, but it was the only venue that was large enough.

Dahtra prepared for her public announcement.

Sam went to his quarters and communicated with his team and Janus telling them what he had agreed to do.

Janus asked if Sam wanted his help.

"I want to try to defeat him without your intervention, Janus. We cannot be seen using what would appear as trickery of some kind. Be ready, though. I don't want to die."

The rest of the team protested, and Sam told them it had to be done.

"I would appreciate it if you could come to the surface to support and watch me. The Satran agreed to this. Contact the Satran's office to make the arrangements. Now I have to concentrate on my Kata, prepare myself mentally, and rest."

* * *

The next morning arrived quickly. The Satran's announcement had drawn an enormous crowd. Sam had asked for a Rocaran hooded travel cape to use for his short trip from his quarters to the arena.

As he was escorted through the crowd he noted the somber demeanor of the Rocara. The Satran's comments must have stressed the importance of this event to their future. There was no laughing, no rowdy behavior. This was a serious moment in their history, and the Rocara were taking it that way.

Sam was ushered into a dressing room near the arena floor. In the arena the Satran addressed the crowd. She repeated her comments about the event's importance, but she let them know that however this turned out, she had faith in them. She explained the Tezaxt and her right to appoint a champion because of the great mismatch in combat abilities. Then she told them who her champion was. It was then when Sam was led to the arena floor.

He removed his cape which set of a wave of murmurs through the crowd. They quieted when Milan came to the center and addressed them. He called the two combatants to the center to remind them of the rules which included the right to yield instead of die. Then he sent them to the side to get ready. Sam repeated his Kata at that time. When he was done, he looked up to see Carmen, Jesse and Travis sitting next to the Satran in her box. Ahleeto was watching on the screen in Thelika's common room.

"Thanks for coming," he said. Then he concentrated on the event.

When Rulian and Sam came to the center again, Milan was there. He said to begin, and quickly backed away.

"I almost laughed when I saw she had chosen you, soft-skin," Rulian said. "I do not want to kill you, so please yield before this goes too far."

Sam didn't say anything. He raised his hands in front of him, put the palms together and bowed to his opponent. Time slowed for Sam as it always had whenever used his skill to defend himself. The last time had been years ago, but he had kept in shape and practiced.

"You have nothing to say, soft-skin?"

Again, Sam was silent. He watched his opponent prepare for his first move. If it hadn't been in slow motion to Sam's way of seeing it, he wouldn't have time to move, and it would have killed him. Rocara were apparently able to strike with both feet at the same time. Sam moved just in time to avoid being crushed and slashed.

Rulian came at him with arms and legs in constant motion. The Rocara body was far more flexible than a Human body, and Rulian was a blur of action. Sam was able to see everything Rulian threw at him. Such was Sam's skill using his chi, his life-force energy, that most of the time he didn't have to touch his opponent while defending himself, the force of his chi was doing the touching for him. After his first several rushes, it was apparent that Rulian was shocked that the Human was still standing and that he was getting winded.

"Why don't you attack, soft-skin?" Rulian asked, while trying to catch his breath.

"I do not want to hurt you. You cannot win this, Rulian. You will come to know this in a few more minutes when your energy is gone, and you fall to the ground. When that time comes, I implore you to yield. I do not want to kill you."

Instead of answering, Rulian attacked again, this time coming so close to hitting Sam that when Sam defended, he struck Rulian's upper right arm and shattered the bones underneath with his chi. Rulian cried out and backed away. Such an injury would have seriously impaired a Human's ability to continue. For a Rocaran, losing the use of an arm only meant that they had three weapons instead of four. After taking a breath, Rulian came at Sam again.

The fight had only been going on for about eight minutes, but the activity was so intense that Rulian was beginning to show signs of fatigue. Sam was breathing hard as well. Sam's defensive movements might have looked effortless, but they were not. Sam was focused. He knew that one slip up, and he would be dead.

Defending another attack from Rulian, Sam broke Rulian's left wrist. With both arms disabled, Rulian skillfully used his feet to continue the attack. When Sam injured one of Rulian's knees, the Rocaran fell to the ground. He was in great pain but did not show it. Sam stepped over to the fallen Rocaran.

"You have fought well, brave warrior. Please yield."

Rulian shook his head and struggled to raise himself off the floor without success. Sam turned toward the Satran's box. Milan was seated near her.

"The Regional Administrator Rulian Trace is a brave and capable foe. He is down and still will not yield. I do not wish to hurt him further. Will you call the contest to a close and declare the winner?"

"Sam! Behind you!" Carmen shouted in English, too startled to remember to use the implant.

Sam turned just in time to see Rulian attack. Somehow the Rocaran had risen from the floor, and with all his strength rushed Sam with his remaining weapon. His jaws were wide open he was intending to kill Sam with his teeth. Sam had only enough time to raise his hands in front of him and push the Rocaran back with his chi. Rulian flew back and landed on the ground. Sam rushed over to him. Sam knew that in his surprise, he had used too much force. He knelt down next to Rulian. Milan ran out at the same time. He put his hand on Rulian's neck. After a moment, he looked up at Sam.

"I'm sorry my friend. Rulian is dead."

Sam bent his head down, put a hand on his dead foe's chest, and shed tears for Rulian and for himself because he had failed to avoid killing this beautiful, if misdirected, sentient being.

21. Administrator

The Performance Arena, Tetara

Sam felt a hand on his shoulder.

"Sam, it is time to move Rulian's body," Milan said. "Let me call some to carry him away."

Sam looked up. No one in the audience had left. The quiet that filled the arena was complete. He looked at Milan.

"Yes. It is time, but I will carry him. Help me get him up."

Milan looked at Sam. It seemed unlikely that a person as slender as Sam could carry a body as large as Rulian's, but he had already underestimated this strange alien once, and would not do so again. Sam bent down and eased his arms under Rulian. As he was beginning to lift the body, Milan helped a little, but his help wasn't needed. Sam came up and stood erect with Rulian in his arms.

"Where shall we take him, Milan?"

Milan led the way. Such was the impact of the drama they had just witnessed that the crowd didn't move or begin talking among themselves until Sam and Milan had left the arena floor. The spell was broken when the floor was cleared. The audience began shuffling toward the exits, talking in subdued tones. What had just happened? What did it mean? What would the Satran say?

"Wait, my friends," the Satran said. "Please remain a moment longer. Rulian Trace was an important member of our

156

society. Please wait and share a moment of silence in his honor."

Everyone stopped where they were and turned toward the Satran. Dahtra stood erect, with her head slightly bowed and hands at her side. Those close enough to see, witnessed the tears streaming down from her eyes. This was not a person celebrating defeat of an enemy, but one who mourned the loss of a fellow Rocaran. She looked up at her people.

"Thank you. I would have avoided this tragedy if Rulian had allowed it. He strongly held onto his belief that the Rocara should continue as we have in the past, and ultimately died defending that view of our future. We will honor him with a fitting ceremony.

"As sad as this drama has been for all of us, let us not lose the significance of what has happened here today, for it marks the beginning of a new era for all Rocara. As Rulian was strong in his beliefs, we will be strong in our conviction to make this beginning a successful one. Thank you for being here. Thank you also to those who have watched today's event from afar. I will need the support of all of you as we implement the changes I described yesterday, and I give you my solemn promise that I will support you as well."

When she finished, a deafening sound emerged from audience. The Rocara were stomping their feet and shouting a chant. It was the way the Rocara applauded and showed their support.

Dahtra had raised her arms as she came to the end of her remarks to emphasize her points. They fell to her sides now, as she stood still, letting the rousing support of the Rocara flow over her. She let herself imagine that other Rocara watching through their comm screens were standing and stomping and chanting like those before her in the arena. Again, tears came, and she let them flow.

* * *

Sam went to his quarters when he left Rulian's body in Rocaran care. His team contacted him. He thanked them for their thoughts and support but said he would need to be alone for a while. He couldn't tell them how long it would take but said he would let them know after having time to think. His team thought it best to return to Thelika until the impact of what happened in the arena was better known.

Sam closed the door of his quarters shutting out the rest of the world. He went into the room that held a shower and let the warm water sooth him. He had killed. He had to find a way past his remorse, and he knew it would take a while.

After the warm water had done all it could he went into the bedroom and put on clean clothes. He drew some water into a cup from the sink in the kitchen area, drank it slowly, filled the cup again and took it to the sitting room. He sat down, and looked out on the beautiful buildings of Tetara, and stilled his mind, soaking up the silence.

He didn't know how long he had been sitting in the cocoon of nothingness before the room signaled that someone was at the door. He knew he had to answer it but was reluctant to leave his oasis of silence.

He went to the door, opened it and found the Satran, and Administrator Chatrec looking concerned.

"May we come in?" Dahtra asked.

"Of course," Sam said. "Please come in."

He led them to the sitting area.

"Can I get you some water?" Sam asked

"We are fine," Dahtra said. "We saw the effect that Rulian's death had on you. We wanted to come and say that we were sorry that you had to go through that."

"I volunteered."

"You planned to avoid killing him," Milan said, "but Rulian forced you to do it. He did not want to live. He used you to get his wish."

"I know," Sam said. "I know also that I had little time to respond, and that in my rush, I used too much force. I know these things, but...."

"Enough about my sorrow! Today is about the Rocara. It is a tragic way to have to have achieved it, but you must feel your way is clear now, Satran. You can create a new era for your people."

"You have won the opportunity for me to do it, and if the response in the arena is typical among the Rocara, then I have the support I need. I thank you for giving me that. I will do my best to see that it is not wasted."

"I know you weren't looking at it this way," Sam said, "but if I understand the Tezaxt rules correctly, the winner also gains all that the loser owned. So you have increased your wealth as well."

"You're right, Sam," Dahtra said, "that wasn't on my mind, but I don't think you understand the Tezaxt as well as you think."

"What do you mean?" Sam asked.

"Milan, could you explain it to our hero?"

"Sam, the Satran has overcome the challenge to her leadership. Thanks to you she will keep her position. The way you conducted yourself during the combat and at the end when you found Rulian was dead, helped convince the Rocara that they had witnessed a genuine Tezaxt, a deadly ritual not seen for a century or more. Thus, they were at ease accepting the result. All of what you did helped accomplish that, but that is all the Satran is due from the Tezaxt.

"According to long standing Tezaxt tradition, when the challenged individual chooses a champion, and that champion is victorious, the holdings of the defeated challenger go the champion, not his sponsor. You, Sam, receive Rulian's wealth and holdings, not the Satran."

"We know this is a difficult moment for you," Dahtra said. "We also understand that what you have won is problematic since you are not Rocaran and don't live here. We thought you should be aware of it as soon as you were ready to hear it from us."

"Yes, it is awkward, but I appreciate you telling me right away. It would be helpful if you would assign someone to help me understand what this means. If Rulian had a close assistant, I would appreciate having them brought here as well. The word of Rulian's death has already spread across your entire Domain. There will be questions of those who worked with him in his Region. Who should they turn to for direction now that the Regional Administrator for the Tarkan Region is dead?"

Dahtra and Milan looked at each other as if perplexed as to what to do. Dahtra decided it was her task so she should tell him.

"That is one more part of this business that you should know right away," she said. "You not only inherit all Rulian's wealth. You also inherit his title. By Rocaran law, Sam, you are the new Regional Administrator of the Tarkan Region."

22. Taking on Tarkan

Sam's Quarters in the Septcium Tower

Sam looked at Dahtra and Milan who were waiting to see his reaction. He had just become the Human Administrator of a Rocaran region. Interesting! That was his reaction. It was interesting the way things had developed. He was sure that he had been drawn to Perillian to protect the planet. That would be an on-going responsibility. Step-by-step he had now found himself in the middle of Rocaran society going through a major change. He felt that nothing happened by accident. He and his team were meant to be here, at least for a while. He needed to find out why!

"Sam?"

"Yes, Dahtra. Sorry for the delay. This is a lot to take in. Are you sure this is a good idea? If I understand things correctly, when I assume the title of Regional Administrator of the Tarkan Region I also become a member of the Septcium, the governing body of the Rocara. How will the Rocara react? I could be helpful to you, but I don't want my presence, and the presence of others that I would bring in to create more problems for you."

"I understand your concern, and appreciate the thought," she said. "Right now there is an aura surrounding you. You are famous because of the Tezaxt. By winning that ancient Rocaran ritual you have been inserted into our cultural record, have become part of the Rocara.

"The victory is symbolic in another, more subtle way. Rulian was a powerful representative of the old Rocaran Domain. You don't know it, but you are strikingly similar to the Xarta, who we rule over. Your victory over Rulian represents a symbolic ending of the old Rocaran rule.

"If we act quickly to establish you as the new Administrator for the Tarkan Region, it will seem a natural step following the events of today. If we act as if it is also natural that you are a member of the Septcium it won't be questioned. Garan Ratra might raise the issue, but that will be dealt with quickly. As you begin to contribute to the effort of transforming the Domain your position will be strengthened."

Sam thought about what the Satran was saying and found that he agreed with her. His being inserted into Rocaran society at this time might be just the catalyst needed to ensure the success of the Satran's plans for her people. What else it might mean for him and his team he would find out along the way.

"I accept."

Dahtra looked at Milan and they both smiled at Sam.

"Thank you, Sam," Dahtra said. "I will have my assistant, Aluta, help you get started."

"That would be good." Sam said. "Milan, thank you for your help in the arena. Since you are in charge of the Rocaran Military I need to ask you, what is my latitude regarding how they are used in the Tarkan Region?"

The question surprised Chatrec. It sounded like Sam was already making plans.

"What did you have in mind, Sam?"

"I might like to have them provide community services as we go through the change the Satran has in mind. I think demilitarizing the military might be an important symbol of the changing Rocaran role in the lives of those you currently rule."

"I would appreciate you consulting with me in advance, but I agree with the general idea. Some of the military will welcome the change."

"Thank you both," Sam said. "What you have offered me, has taken my mind off the unpleasant aspect of the Tezaxt. Now I need to get to my shuttle and rejoin my team on our ship. I should be back shortly. Would Aluta have time this afternoon to discuss things with me?"

"I'll make sure she is available."

They stood up, and the two Rocara turned toward the door.

"Satran, may I speak with you for a moment?" Sam asked.

Dahtra, nodded, smiled at Milan, and said she would talk with him later. Milan left and she turned to Sam.

"What do you wish to discuss in private, Sam?"

"I think you know that not all Rocara will be in favor of the changes you propose, and that you are potentially in danger. I wanted to let you know that we will be watching to assure your safety in addition to the guards you might plan to have around you. We have the ability to stop violence before it happens without resorting to violence."

The Satran looked at Sam, not understanding. Sam couldn't tell her anymore. He didn't want to talk about telepathy, teleportation, Janus and the rest, but they might need to put someone to sleep if they intended harm. He had to prepare her.

"I know this is confusing. I wish I could tell you more. I'm telling you this much, so you won't be shocked when we act. We will be watching out for you. If someone surprisingly collapses around you, please know that person had intended to harm you or someone near you. They won't be dead, just asleep. Have them confined. Act as if the person had a seizure and needed to be cared for. Put a guard on the person and contact me."

"Can you tell me more now?"

"No, Satran, I cannot. Please trust me. It might never come up, but I wanted you to be prepared if it does."

"Alright, Sam. I trust you. I hope you will be able to trust me enough to tell me about this sometime in the future."

"We'll see. Thank you," Sam said.

Sam asked for a way to contact her quickly if he needed to. Dahtra gave him the information and assigned a person to lead Sam to his HSHP. He eased it off of the landing pad using the fans. He contacted his team aboard Thelika, lifted the craft well up in the atmosphere before he teleported the HSHP inside Thelika's hold.

He met his team in the common room. The last they had heard from him was that he needed time to get over what had happened in the arena. His level of energy when he came into the room was much higher than they expected.

"Looks like you're over the earlier event," Jesse said, when Sam had found a seat among them.

"I have been able to push it to the back of my mind, but it will take time to deal with it completely. I've been able to set it aside because of what the Rocara have told me."

Sam told them about the Rocaran Domain, that the Rocara were governed by the Septcium who ruled over a number of native people on numerous planets in the Domain. He also told them about the Satran and her plan for change, and what he had just found out about his victory in the Tezaxt.

"Awkward," Carmen said.

"Amazing," Jesse said.

"What can we do to help?" Travis asked.

"Ahleeto, what do you think about it?" Sam asked.

"It sounds like another interesting assignment for the team," she answered. "I hope I can be included in some way."

"Thanks, Ahleeto and all of you," Sam said. "I will need your help. I've been thinking non-stop since I learned I would be the new Administrator. I have ideas, and know that I will also need Martha, Thelika and Janus to be in on this as well.

"I was beginning to wonder if you had forgotten I was aboard," Martha said.

"Never," Sam said. "The same goes for you Thelika. There is something I need to set up before we go on.

"Janus, could you watch over the Satran? I've told her we will be watching out for her and what it meant if someone suddenly collapses to the floor near her. I didn't tell her about you, or how it was done."

"I've begun the watch, Sam, and I agree that we shouldn't discuss me with the Rocara at this time."

"I also think we should keep telepathy and teleportation behind the veil," Sam said. "It might be difficult. We can use them, but we have to be discreet about it."

He looked at the group. They seemed excited at the prospect, but they also had seen so much in their work together that this didn't seem overwhelming. They were ready to discuss how to get it done.

"What's our objective, Sam?" Carmen asked.

"Excellent way to get this started," he said. "We will be working mostly within the region I have been assigned, but my hope is that the changes we introduce in that region will influence the rest of the Domain. The overall objective that I have is to help the Rocara and those they rule through the transition from empire to self-rule, and to help them establish some form of a federation of equals. I want your input on this, but that's what I see."

"What about Perillian and that assignment?" Janus asked. "Are we done there?"

"Are you getting any more input from your friend-of-few-words?" Jesse asked.

"I have not received words, but 'feelings.' The feeling I have is that the job at Perillian is not done. We should continue to focus on it, but we have achieved the initial purposes of learning about the planet and that it has to be protected. Protection is an on-going responsibility, but with the Rocara turned aside we have dealt with the initial concern. I also have the feeling that there is more to learn there, but I think we knew that."

"Thanks, Janus," Sam said. "That's what I've been thinking about Perillian. Okay. There are numerous facets of this Rocaran project that need to be addressed all at the same time. There are two sentient races in my new region. I'll work with the Ortari. They won't think that anything important has changed. On their level of perception I agree with them. Carmen and Jesse, I'll work with you, but I would like you to work with the other one, the Batani.

"I have inherited a great deal of Rocaran wealth. The questions are how much is there and what should we do with it? I think an assessment of the total enterprise of the Tarkan Region is part of this as well. I will have to recruit someone for this task. Martha, I think you will be needed here as well."

"What about Kristen for that one?" Jesse suggested. "She's been running Compass Enterprises for you for some time. She's good at what she does and might be looking for a new assignment."

"Good idea, Jesse. I'll contact her when we are done. The next one I'd like you to work on, Travis. I have the feeling that with labor so cheap and readily available from the Domain's subjects, the Rocara have not innovated much in their mines and factories. I would like to free them to work on higher level tasks if they want to."

"That sounds like fun," Travis said, "but I could use a good engineer to work with."

Jesse spoke up again.

"Thornton Rodgers might be a good fit. He does engineering analysis for Compass, and he is married to Kristen.

She might like the assignment even more if Thornton could be here with her."

"Another good idea, Jesse," Sam said.

"Ahleeto, I think it might be helpful for you to be in on negotiations of one sort or another as we go along" Sam said. "Right now, I'd like you and Thelika to think about how we will be transporting team members, Rocara and others, and supplies around during the project."

"Yes," Ahleeto said. "With this many different activities in five-star systems, I think we will need as many as two more Lorengi ships. I will have them come here."

"Thank you. I have arranged to talk with the Satran's assistant this afternoon. I would like you to come with me and have Thelika, Martha and Janus listening in. We'll leave in about an hour, if that's okay."

Sam looked at his team. They were excited, and apparently not the least troubled about all that they did not know at this point.

"I need to contact a couple of people. I'll meet you back here when it's time to leave."

He got up and went to his quarters. He left the others talking about what was to come. He contacted Kristen first. She sounded enthusiastic about the prospect of an off-planet assignment. She said she would talk with Thornton and get back to Sam. His next communication was with his wife, Lesley.

"Hi, Les."

"Ah, my wandering husband. Where in the galaxy are you?"

"Far, far away. I wanted to call you to let you know that I, uh, won't be home for dinner."

23. Welcomed

Planet Tarka, Rocaran Complex

Aluta had told Sam that Kemel Bosin had been Rulian's chief of staff. After teleporting in Thelika to Earth to pick up Kristen and Thornton, Sam made arrangements to meet with Bosin the next day. He and his team arrived at the main Rocaran complex early morning, local Tarkan time and flew over the complex in the HSHP to get an overview.

The buildings were flat-roofed, had two floors, and were colored in greens and tans that matched the surrounding forest. Some of the buildings appeared to be quarters for Rocara assigned to Tarkan, others were office buildings. There were two hangers where locally needed equipment and air cars were located.

Sam parked the HSHP in the larger of the two hangers. Three Rocara met them there. All three wore short-sleeved, tan uniforms, which contrasted nicely with the light-green color of their scales. When the Human team exited the HSHP, one of the Rocara came up to them and introduced himself as Kemel.

"They seem apprehensive and curious, but otherwise at ease," Janus told the team.

"Welcome to Tarkan, Administrator Baxter," Kemel said. "Let us go to the main building where we can answer your questions and help you with your responsibilities."

Ahleeto's arrival next to the Humans gave the Rocara a shock. Sam explained her presence and appearance. That helped, but they remained wary.

The entrance to the main building had a sign identifying it as Rocaran Headquarters and was more impressive than the other buildings. Kemel led them to a meeting room on the second level. Large windows were along one of the walls, providing a view of the forest.

Sam sat down at the head of the long oval table. Carmen, Travis, Jesse, Kristen, Thornton and Ahleeto sat across from Kemel and his two assistants. Introductions were made. One of Kemel's assistants, a female Rocara, was an engineer. The other was male and was the head of the finance section. There were containers of water on the table. Sam filled one of the cups and took a sip. There was an uncomfortable moment of silence. Sam spoke to get things started.

"Thank you, Kemel, for being ready for us. Could you tell me how the Rocara are feeling about the loss of Rulian Trace and my taking over?"

"That is an awkward question, Administrator Baxter," Kemel said. "Are you expecting me to be candid?"

"Not if it makes you uncomfortable," Sam said. "I merely point out that having me take over, someone who is not Rocaran, might be difficult to accept. I'd like to know if I will meet resistance."

Kemel looked at the two Rocara next to him and then back at Sam.

"Administrator Trace was…uh…difficult to work for," Kemel said, obviously choosing his words carefully. "I believe the Rocara in the Tarkan region will welcome the change. As for your not being Rocaran it is understood that though this is an unusual situation your Tezaxt victory places you in this role."

Sam thought this was a good start. He decided he had his answer.

"Thank you for your candid response, Kemel. Let me describe my immediate plans and the roles of those I have brought with me."

Sam noted the Rocara reactions as he told them what he wanted done and how fast he wanted the assessment and analysis tasks completed. They were surprised, but not overwhelmed.

"You will have the Rocara you need to help you," Kemel said. "May I ask what your objectives are, Administrator Baxter?"

"My first objective is to quickly find out all about the Tarkan Region. I will then begin to make changes that I think will improve conditions for everyone in the Region and will increase efficiency of production. I also will be implementing the Satrans plans for self-rule for the natives in the Region."

"If I may observe, Administrator, the self-rule for our subjects in the Tarkan Region will present interesting challenges," Kemel said, smiling.

"Could you explain?" Carmen asked.

Kemel looked at Sam as if not sure whether to answer Carmen directly. Sam thought that perhaps staff was not to speak unless spoken to in the past under Rulian. Sam decided that it was a good time to clarify matters.

"Kemel, we are very informal about protocol. Everyone joins in the conversation when discussing things. Also, it might be difficult for you to change how you address me, but I would prefer that you call me by my first name, Sam."

Kemel looked shocked at first and then relieved.

"Thank you, Sam. Administrator Trace had very strict rules about this. Now to answer your question, Carmen, in addition to the Rocara, there two different races in this Region. The Ortari on this planet do not seem to recognize that we are ruling them. I still do not understand that. They probably will not recognize that we have switched to self-rule either."

"I believe I understand the situation," Sam said. "I plan to talk with the Ortari."

Sam's comment brought another surprised look to Kemel's face, but he went on.

"On planet Eltan the native people are called the Batani. The challenge there will be to get them to accept self-rule, or at least that will be the case with the more affluent Batani. The poor might want the change. It is the less fortunate Batani who have been actively opposing the Rocara.

"The wealthy Batani have worked themselves into the local government. Others own or run certain businesses and have the poorer Batani working for them. The rich Batani have become rich and comfortable under Rocaran rule. I do not think they would welcome a change unless they could be assured of maintaining their current position.

"Thank you, Kemel," Carmen said. "Jesse and I would welcome your insights as we approach making changes on Eltan. I believe what we have in mind for the Batani may make the wealthy Batani uncomfortable."

Sam could see the three Rocara at the table relax. Without his instigation, conversations began flying back and forth across the table. Kristen was having an animated conversation with the finance manager. Travis was having the same kind of discussion with the Rocaran engineer.

"Kemel, are there others that we will need to work with that should be in these conversations?"

"Yes, Sam. I will have different discussions taken to separate rooms, and make sure the right Rocara are involved in each. I will be joining Carmen and Jesse to discuss their plans for the Batani," Kemel said. "First, let me show you the Administrator's office, and introduce you to your assistant."

Sam's assistant was a Rocaran female named Nelai Tontu. Sam tried to introduce Nelai to his more relaxed form of working together. She didn't change her formality, but she did seem relieved finding that Sam wasn't the tyrant that Rulian was. Nelai reminded Sam of Stephanie who was the office manager at Compass Enterprises years ago. Stephanie always spoke formally when addressing Sam and his friend Jeff Pierce.

Sam let Kemel go back to work with the others. He asked Nelai about the Ortari. She seemed unused to being consulted on anything and was slow to answer him.

"I don't know very much about them. What I hear is that they are primitive in their living habits, but not an ignorant people. Perhaps they just enjoy living simply."

"Thank you, Nelai. Are there Ortari all over the planet or just in a few areas?"

"I have never been told. I am only familiar with the settlement not too far from our complex."

"Could you tell me where they are? I plan to go there this morning."

She was surprised that the Regional Administrator would wish to visit the Ortari but told him how far away they were. Having translated Rocaran measurements into Human ones before, it seemed that the nearest community was about thirty miles from the complex near the shore of a small lake. Nelai said an air car would be made available for him.

"You aren't planning to go by yourself are you, Administrator?"

"Yes, I'll be fine as long as I follow your directions."

"But, Administrator Trace always had a driver and guard accompany him when traveling on the planet."

"I will use the shuttle we brought with us, so I won't need a driver, and I don't need a guard."

Nelai took Sam to the hanger. She introduced Sam and explained his plans to the Rocaran in charge of the equipment.

Sam went to the HSHP. He told Nelai to tell Kemel and Sam's people where he went, and that he would be back in a while. He started the HSHP, raising a bit of dust. The two Rocara backed away. Sam moved the craft out of the hanger and up over the nearby forest. He hoped he had understood Nelai's correctly because from the air, the forest looked the same in all directions.

He flew at low speed in the direction Nelai had given him, not wanting to miss anything that might confirm he was going the right way. A short time after leaving the complex, Sam thought he could see the sunlight reflecting off of what could be the surface of a lake. He took a chance that it was a lake and the one he was looking for and headed towards it.

A few minutes later he was over the lake. He looked around for something that would indicate a settlement of some kind. He spotted a few canoe-like boats on the shore on the far side of the lake. Near the boats was a spot where the forest had been cleared. He decided that was what he was looking for and landed in the clearing inland from the shore.

As he expected a small contingent of the native Ortari was there to greet him. With what he believed he understood about their perception of things in the universe, they would know he was coming.

The Ortari reminded him of the Agara on Perillian. They were just over five feet high and covered in short brown fur, had large foreheads, and instead of hair, the rest of their head was covered by fur. Their faces were fur-less, and flat with a short nose and a thin mouth below it. Their eyebrows were bushy above large round eyes that seemed to take in everything around them. They wore simple garments, tunics over pants, which looked like they were woven from a plant-based fabric.

Sam walked up to the group of Ortari and said hello in Rocaran.

"Welcome, Sam, we have been waiting for you," an Ortari in front of the group said, "My name is Artis."

"Thank you, Artis. I would like to learn about the Ortari, Artis. Would that be alright with you?"

"Of course. Let us go to our village."

Sam and the Ortari walked the short distance to the compound just inside the forest. There was a circle of twenty huts with a neatly landscaped clearing in the center, where the sun shone brightly. The other Ortari of the community came out and formed a circle. Artis led Sam to one side of the circle, and they sat down with the others. All eyes were on Sam.

He remembered the description of Herata's visit with this community. The Ortari had barely acknowledged her. Sam doubted the difference in his greeting was because of his newly attained post as the head of the local Rocaran government. So he had to wonder what was different. Artis gave him the answer.

"Will you tell us about the planet that thinks, and what you know of the Urritan?" Artis asked.

24. The Ortari

Planet Tarka, Ortari Village

Herata Demis, the Rocaran Administrator, had told Sam that the Ortari had spoken of the "awakening planet," which the Urritan had called Perillian. He was surprised that the Ortari also knew of the Urritan.

"Herata, your recent visitor, said that you mentioned something new was awakening," Sam said. "Could you tell me how you became aware of that?"

"We listen," Artis said.

A bit cryptic, Sam thought, so he pursued it further.

"Can you show me how you listen?"

Artis looked at him in disbelief. Was it because he didn't think it was possible to teach Sam this, or was the look one of surprise that Sam couldn't 'listen' as the Ortari did?

"It was thought that you would already know how to listen," Artis said.

"Perhaps I do," Sam said, glad to get the answer to his quandary. "I'm just not familiar with it being called 'listening.' Could you lead me into your method?"

Another quizzical look from Artis, and then a nod of acceptance.

"Close your eyes, Sam, and join with us."

Sam closed his eyes and found himself surrounded by a mass of brightness, which was the consciousness emanating from the circle of Ortari. He calmed himself, and listened only with his mind, shutting out any sounds from the outside. Then he understood that yes, he had the ability, but hadn't focused the way the Ortari did. Joining with them gave him that focus, and he heard/saw/felt what they meant.

There was what Sam could only describe as "energy" of some type surrounding and passing through everything everywhere. He could then understand that if one were very familiar with the normal pattern of this energy, anything different, like a planet "waking," would stand out.

He joined with the Ortari as they reached out with their perception across vast distances of the surrounding galaxy. There were points of luminescence enmeshed in the flow. He understood from his work with Janus that all matter had consciousness, but in a view such as his mind saw now, only the stronger consciousness of beings stood out. This view of reality was similar to what Carmen had showed him, but with the addition of the energy field.

The Ortari stopped the expansion of their view at what Sam thought must be a planet. He guessed it to be Perillian. The Ortari increased the resolution of their view so that Sam was able to distinguish different sources of consciousness on the planet. Agar the AI below the surface, the Teratta, Agara and Agarians each had their own pattern of consciousness in this view. Separate from them and surrounding them all was a bright, glowing light around the entire planet.

After the deep silence of thought that Sam had been experiencing on this journey, it was a shock when Artis communicated with him telepathically.

"The glow around the planet is a recent development," Artis said. *"Do you understand, now?"*

"Yes," Sam said.

"Then let us return to our village."

Sam opened his eyes and saw the solidity of the Ortari village and surrounding forest. The difference was startling.

"Thank you, Artis," Sam said. "You were right assuming that I have the ability. I just needed to learn how to use it. It will take practice to develop it to the extent the Ortari have, but I will never forget how to do it."

"You're welcome, Sam. We are honored to be able to share the experience with you, being who you are. Could you tell us about the planet that wakes, now?"

Sam didn't miss the reference to his importance. Just another thing for which he would have to wait for an answer. He set it aside and told them what he knew of the planet Perillian and the three sentient races on it.

"That explains three of the sources of consciousness on the planet," Artis said. "We sensed a fourth."

"Yes. It is an artificial intelligence that was put in place by the Urritan to manage the planet. The Urritan had shaped the land into three separate continents filled with the Teratta, large tree-like beings who developed self-awareness after a million years of existence."

"What do you mean?" Artis asked. "Are you saying that after thousands of generations of the Teratta, the new ones began to develop self-awareness?"

Sam would not tell anyone else what he was about to tell the Ortari, but he knew it was safe with them.

"No, Artis. The Teratta are two million years old. After they had lived a million years, they began to develop self-awareness."

"Interesting."

"We thought so as well. We wanted to find out how it was possible. One of the Teratta allowed us to use our instruments to look inside of it so we could find out how it was done."

Sam went on to tell them what they found.

"Extraordinary. You say the Teratta were designed that way, by the Urritan?"

"Yes."

"So that is how they did it," Artis said, causing Sam to wonder what he meant. "What about the other two races?"

"They were created by the AI. In our view, the consciousness of the Agara and Agarians had little impact on what developed there. We believe that it was the over one hundred billion, self-aware Teratta that may have been what triggered the planet's awakening."

Artis and other Ortari nodded their heads, understanding why Sam came to that conclusion.

"Why did the Urritan do all of this?" Artis asked.

"The AI on the planet said the Urritan reshaped the planet to be a garden for the Urritan to visit. Apparently, they never returned to enjoy the result."

"What do you know of the Urritan, Sam?"

"Only what we learned by talking with the AI and looking around the chamber in which it was enclosed. They were advanced technologically, and about twice my size. Everything else we might think about them would be speculation."

"Why did you go there in the first place?" Artis asked.

"What do you think, Janus? Should I tell the Ortari about you and your friend?"

Sam had a communications link to Janus through Martha. He could speak out loud, Janus picked up his thoughts and responded through Sam's implant. When Sam wanted the conversation to be private, he used telepathy, which could be directed selectively to only the desired recipient.

"They are a people who would be able to grasp what I am, and we might learn something about my new 'friend-of-few-words' as Jesse calls it."

Sam agreed and told the Ortari about Janus. Janus went on to introduce himself to them and provide a more complete description of what he was.

"Thank you, Sam. That helps explain what we have been wondering about," Artis said.

Sam looked at the other Ortari. They were nodding and had looks of understanding on their faces.

A different look appeared on Sam's face. He wondered what they meant. What had they been wondering about? Who were the Ortari? He decided to ask his last question first.

"Artis, are there other Ortari on this planet?"

"No, Sam. We are the only Ortari. There are no others on this planet or any other planet, except those few who were taken away by the Rocara to work in mines elsewhere."

"Had there been more of you in some earlier time?"

"Yes, but not many more."

Sam looked around at the circle of Ortari. There were three children in the group, so perhaps the birth-life-death cycle here was more like he was used to than it was on Perillian. Still, how could a race made up of so few members sustain itself?

"You have questions, Sam," Artis said. It was a statement not a question.

"Yes. In my limited understanding of biology, there needs to be a larger number of members in a race than you have here for the race to sustain itself over time. Yet here you are."

"Our 'biology' is different from what you have studied on your home world," Artis said. "Like the Teratta, we were created this way by the Urritan. They were better at their craft than the AI they had put on Perillian. We are not automatons with limited functionality like the two races the AI created on Perillian. As you have seen, the Ortari are functioning with a higher level of understanding and freedom of action."

Sam was astounded. He didn't know what question to ask next, but he stumbled on with the next question that came to mind.

"You said that my description of how we were drawn to Perillian explained some things for you. What were they?"

"There have been powerful emanations from our planet recently. We didn't understand what they were or why it was happening. We think we understand now."

Sam let that go for the moment. Something was nagging at the back of his mind.

"Why did the Urritan create you?"

"They were a lonely race," Artis said. "We were created to be companions they could talk with. We were not creatures at their level, but we understood enough so they might have reasonable conversations with us."

"If they wanted you as companions, why did they leave you here?" Sam asked.

Artis looked at the circle of Ortari, and then back at Sam.

"They didn't leave us here, Sam. This is where we were created and have been since the beginning. This is the Urritan home world."

"Don't you mean 'was' the home world of the Urritan?"

"I suppose that is also correct," Artis said, contemplatively, "but it still is their home world."

"What do you mean?" Sam asked. "It isn't like they are still living here."

"That depends on your definition of living," Artis said. "The Urritan became part of the systems below the surface when they learned that as a live, organic race they were doomed. It was the Urritan in the systems below who created the emanations. We now wonder if those emanations might have been sent to your kind."

25. Back to Business

"Janus?"

"This is interesting, Sam. I get the feeling that whatever is below on this planet is waiting for us."

"It will have to wait a bit longer. We have things we need to do for the Rocara and others."

"I understand. I think it does as well," Janus confirmed

"Sam?" Artis said to get Sam's attention.

"Yes, Artis. What you have said is very interesting. Thank you."

"No thanks are necessary, Sam. The Urritan know of you. It will be an honor to help if we can."

"Do you know how to enter the sub-surface chambers of the Urritan?"

"We know where to enter, but we have not been given the ability to enter. Perhaps you will be able to."

"You might be right," Sam said, "but that will have to wait. My team and I have made commitments to the Rocara which we will have to address before we explore this any further. The Rocara have given me authority over this planet. That means I can stop any further intrusions."

"That is a good thing," Artis said. "The Rocara have been here for some time but haven't bothered anything important. I don't know for certain, but I believe the Urritan have taken measures to protect their facilities. Such protections have not been needed up to now. Since you are here, I can see they won't be needed in the future."

"Thank you for your confidence. I have to leave for a while. Those who came with me and I will be back to continue this discussion."

"We will be waiting," Artis said. "We are very pleased you are here and look forward to what will come next. It has been a long time since anything important has happened on this world. For your information, the name of this world is not Tarka as the Rocara refer to it. The Urritan called it Merillian. Welcome to Merillian."

Sam thought about what "a long time" must mean in the Ortari's long existence as he walked back to the HSHP. It may mean a span of time that reached back to Sam's own race's sketchy beginning.

When he arrived at the Rocaran complex he didn't tell his team what he had discovered. Instead he brought his team, Kemel and his two Rocaran assistants back into the larger meeting room and asked them what they had done so far. It had only been three hours, but it looked like they were bursting with information they wanted to share. He asked Kristen to go first.

"By examining the records here I've learned that the wealth you inherited is enormous. About half of it is real estate in Tetara, and partial ownership of some Rocaran companies. The rest is more liquid. Apparently being a Regional Administrator gives one the opportunity to gain wealth like being a government leader on Earth. It's massive."

"That is good to hear, Kristen," Sam said. "I think Travis and Thornton may have use for some of it."

"You're right, Sam," Travis said. "We have found what you suspected. Mining and manufacturing are labor intensive. Thornton and I have already spotted ways to improve things. Some improvements won't need much capital, but to get the more substantial changes, we'll need to put in new equipment. With our understanding of similar facilities on Earth we will be able to use things we've already invented. To do that we will have to manufacture equipment in the Tarkan Region. That will be a drain on our existing capital, but there will be a great return from the more efficient operations. In addition, once the other Regions see the benefits, they will be asking us to make similar equipment for them."

Sam was pleased to hear what he expected, but it raised a caution.

"You aren't planning to put any manufacturing on this planet are you?"

"Nope," Travis said. "We need workers in the factories. We'll put it on Eltan, where coincidently our new equipment will be eliminating their former jobs. The manufacturing jobs will be those 'higher level' jobs you spoke of. The Batani will need some training, but I've been talking about that with Carmen."

"Carmen?"

"Yes, those jobs with higher wages are an important part of what I believe we will be doing on Eltan. There is a definite economic stratification on Eltan. The rich get richer by using the poor, whose standard of living keeps slipping lower. We will set up a system of government on Eltan to improve things for the poorer Batani. Jesse, Kemel and I have already started designing it. Of course we will modify to fit what we find when we get there."

"I thought we were going to let them rule themselves," Sam said.

"We will," Carmen said, "but before we, as the Rocaran management, can implement self-rule on Eltan, we have to be assured that the Batani government that is put in place is stable and sustainable. If we just turn it over to the Batani, the rich will put themselves in control, and the downtrodden will not fare well.

"The less fortunate Batani have been actively resisting Rocaran rule. If the rich Batani take over from the Rocara, there will be uprisings, and people will get hurt. We'll set up Rocaran oversight as the fledgling government gets going and keep it in place until we know it is stable.

"What about taxation to pay for the government?" Kristen asked.

"The Rocara already collect taxes on Eltan," Kemel answered. "It will be kept in place to implement the taxes the new government establishes and have the Batani take it over as time goes on. The difference will be that the tax revenues will go into the Batani treasury instead of flowing back to the Domain."

"I'd like to present a solution to the Septcium for the changes in this Region that the Domain can afford," Sam said. "Kristen, have you found out what types and amounts of revenues are flowing from this Region back to the Domain?"

"Revenues flow from operations on all planets in the system through the Region Headquarters here and then to the Domain," Kristen said.

She stopped there and looked at Kemel.

"Kemel, please don't be offended. I'm just reporting what I have learned."

"I think I know what you are about to say," Kemel said. "What you found is that not all of the revenue from this Region gets to the Domain Treasury. That may or may not be the practice in other regions, but it was one of the ways that Administrator Trace added to his wealth. He was the only one who benefited from the practice, so none of the rest of us will be offended by your report."

"Thank you, Kemel," Kristen said. "Sam, it looks like Trace took ten percent of the revenue for himself. We can use the revenue we will gain from eliminating that practice to help pay for the changes in the Region.

"What about Tarka, Kristen?" Sam asked.

"There is not much profit generated on Tarka. It is mostly an expense to the Domain which covers the management of the Regional Headquarters. It will be lower in the future as we reduce the Rocaran staff in the transition to self-rule.

"Travis have you had a chance to look at Rocaran operations on Tarka?" Sam asked

"Yes."

"How long would it take to clean them up and shut them down? By clean up, I mean restore the ground to something close to what it was before the Rocara came."

"I've only seen video images of the sites, but I think it can be done in six months.'"

" Good," Sam said. "Kristen, assume you will be phasing out all Rocaran activity on Tarka. Ask Travis for the cleanup costs. As for the Regional Headquarters, keep it in your plan for now."

The last part drew a sharp look from Kemel. Sam's crew looked at Sam wondering what he had in mind.

"What about the future for the Headquarters, Sam?" Kemel asked.

"I don't know that yet, Kemel. I want to work with you on that. I won't make any decisions about it without you being involved. I know that leaves you with less certainty than you might like."

Kemel smiled. "Although your comments point toward a possible big change, what you have just said about my involvement, offers more certainty than we have had in our day-to-day interactions with Administrator Trace."

Sam laughed as did the rest of the table including the Rocara.

"Kristen, my comments about Tarka got us distracted from my original question," Sam said. "Will the revenue flowing to the Domain decrease, increase, or remain the same from the changes we are talking about?"

"It's too early to be certain," Kristen said. "I've only had this afternoon to look at it, Sam. I believe that using the former Administrator's ten percent skim to offset the additional costs making changes in the Region will keep the revenue to the Domain at about the same level."

"That's good enough for now. I appreciate your assessment and the work all of you have done and that of the others you have involved in this first look. Well done. Thanks!"

The Humans were pleased with the praise. The Rocara didn't know what to do with it. When Sam looked at Kemel, the Rocaran gave him the answer.

"Those are the first words of praise we have had since we began working here, Sam," Kemel said. "We don't know how to respond."

It didn't take long for the Rocara to adjust. They began smiling along with their Human counterparts.

Sam asked if they had taken time to eat. It turned out that Kemel had the staff in the dining facility provide food in the meeting rooms. Sam was too keyed up to think about food for himself. He asked Kemel if there was a place that he and his team could sit outside and talk. Kemel directed them to an open courtyard in the middle of the complex. When they arrived there, they found it was well landscaped, with trees providing shade over a comfortable seating area.

Sam let the natural conversations go on for a while. They gradually died out, and everyone looked at him. It was time.

"Kristen, Janus said that he had told you and Thornton about how we were drawn out to this part of the galaxy in the first place. Do you have any questions about that?"

"No, Sam. We understood what Janus said. Since then, we've talked with the others about their experiences on Perillian."

"Good, we'll take it from there," Sam said. "I visited with the Ortari today. I haven't had time to investigate what I learned, but I thought I better tell you about it as soon as possible. The first we heard of an ancient race called the Urritan was on Perillian. I heard more about the Urritan when I visited the Ortari today."

Sam let that settle, pausing a moment adding to the drama.

"The AI Agar on Perillian said something about them being stored in a way similar to you, Ahleeto," Sam said.

"Stored? Where?" Travis asked.

"On their home world," Sam said, smiling.

"Where is their home world?" Thornton asked.

Thornton was a little taller than Kristen, and had a thin, somewhat bony frame. Thornton had been quiet in the short time he had been with the team. Sam was glad to see he was beginning to relax within the group.

"Sam, darn it, stop teasing us," Carmen said.

"You're right Carmen. I'm having way too much fun with this. The Ortari told me that we are sitting on the home world of the Urritan, which they called Merillian! On Perillian, we were told that the Urritan had been absent for two million years. The Ortari just told me that the chamber that houses the digitally stored Urritan is right under the Ortari settlement about thirty miles from here!"

26. The Batani

The City of Rotahra on the Planet Eltan

Kemel accompanied Sam and his team on their trip to Eltan. Kemel knew the Rocaran who managed the planet and was familiar with the history of Rocaran rule of the Batani. When they arrived in orbit around Eltan, they took two HSHPs to the principal city of the Batani, Rotahra. The Rocaran manager, Ilanni Tone, met them at the shuttle port which was walking distance from the Rocaran headquarters for the planet.

Ilanni, a female Rocaran, wore a dark green blouse over cream-colored slacks. The dark green of the blouse accentuated the light green of her facial scales, and the grey-green of her eyes. She smiled as she approached. She seemed business-like to Sam but the twinkle in her eye seemed to indicate she had a sense of humor and found the current situation interesting. Sam thought he would like working with her.

Two other Rocara and one rotund Batani accompanied the planet manager.

"Welcome to Eltan, Administrator Baxter," Ilanni said. "I am Ilanni Tone, Rocaran Manager of the planet Eltan. The speed of your trip from Tarka almost didn't allow us time to arrange to meet you when you landed."

"Thank you for working us into your busy day," Sam said.

"It is never a problem to make time for the Regional Administrator," Ilanni said. "Allow me to introduce the Batani City Manager, Amdar Lid."

Amdar came forward and bowed slightly at the waist in greeting. Sam did the same.

"Good to meet you Ser Lid," Sam said, in Rocaran. The Batani language was still spoken in homes and Batani conversations, but Rocaran was the language used in all important matters. One addressed male Batani as "Ser" and female Batani as "Sera."

"A pleasure, Administrator Baxter."

Ilanni also introduced her two aides and then led them toward Rocaran headquarters. A small group of Batani commoners had formed on the plaza near the front door. They were dressed simply in worn but clean garments. Now that Sam had the opportunity to see more than one Batani, he was able to complete his picture of what the Batani looked like.

They varied in height, but the average appeared to be about five-foot six. None of the Batani in the group had the city manager's wide girth. Those in the group were thin, bordering on gaunt. Most had dark brown or black hair. Their thin arms were proportionately longer than on a Human, as were their legs. The result was a rather short-looking body core section. Their facial feature set them apart from any race Sam had seen so far. They had narrow heads, with a face that jutted out. The long, bony nose completed the look that was almost bird-like. It looked as if their eyes were forward just enough on the face that they would still be able to have stereoscopic vision like humans. What saved the overall effect from being unattractive were their warm smiles.

The City Manager was not smiling. Sam guessed that the City manager's frown might be because of the group's presence.

One of the Batani from the group stepped forward.

"Do I have the pleasure of meeting the new Rocaran Administrator?" the Batani asked.

The City Manager moved as if he were going to block the Batani's access to Sam. Sam was faster.

"Yes, I am Administrator, Sam Baxter. May I know your name?"

The City Manager began to speak, again trying to avoid further contact. One look from Sam stopped him.

"My name is Hocan Duar. I am here with my friends to request an audience with you."

"I agree we should meet. I would like to learn your view of things, Ser Duar. I will be meeting with Ilanni Tone and the City Manager for a time. Could we meet after that? Will you be available then?"

The Rocara and the City Manager were obviously surprised at Sam's offer. The smiles of the Batani in the group broadened, obviously pleased that their request had been granted so readily. Other emotions were visible as well. Ilanni Tone and her assistants were smiling, Amdar Lid was furious.

Amdar could control himself no longer. "Duar how dare you approach us in this manner. You shall be dealt with." After having released his pent-up feeling, the City Manager realized his mistake. He tried to say something to cover his blunder, but the looks on the Rocaran and Human faces showed everyone had noticed his inappropriate outburst.

Sam smiled.

"Perhaps, Ser Duar, we should meet with you first," Sam said, "so you are not lost to us by whatever Ser Lid has in mind for you."

"That won't be necessary, Administrator," Ilanni said, smiling. "The City Manager might be upset, but I assure you, nothing will happen to Ser Duar or his friends. In fact, one of my aides will bring them to a room inside and provide them refreshments while they wait."

Surprise upon surprise registered on the faces of the Batani. That something very different from what the Batani were used to was happening here was evident to the Humans. It was a beginning.

Ilanni led Sam and the others into a small meeting room. The room had windows providing a view of a park near the building, so it didn't feel as cramped as it might otherwise. There was a slim rectangular table in the room. Ilanni pointed Sam toward the head of the table. He took the suggestion. The local Rocara and the City manager sat on one side, Sam's team and Kemel sat on the other.

The City Manager had apparently decided that after his blunder he had nothing to lose now by proceeding without tact. Besides being an impulsive individual, Amdar seemed to be emboldened by the announcement that the Rocara were going to move to self-rule for the Batani.

"The Batani would like to know about your plans after the announcement from the Satran, Administrator Baxter," Ser Lid said.

"We are here to begin discussions on several matters, Ser Lid. Perhaps we can begin with introductions, and then move on to the agenda for this preliminary meeting."

Sam had brought all of his core team with him and introduced each of them. Sam then told the group about what they planned for Eltan.

"We will want to meet with numerous Batani in all parts of the planet but thought starting here would be a good idea."

Amdar tried to speak again. Sam held up his hand.

"Ilanni, can you arrange an itinerary that would allow us to meet with a broad cross section of Batani society right away?"

"Yes. We will have suggestions ready for you before the end of the day," Ilanni said.

"Why ask Ilanni Tone to tell you who to meet with?" Amdar asked. "I am known around our world. I can connect you with all the right Batani."

"We will certainly consider your suggestions, Ser Lid," Sam said. "We will also want the ideas from Ilanni and her staff, and from others, like Ser Duar, who you dealt with rather rudely."

"He deserved no better," Amdar said. "He has been causing trouble for a long time now. When we take over we will deal with people like him."

"You just can't help yourself, can you?" Carmen asked, smiling.

"What do mean?" Amdar asked.

"Here you are in front of the Rocaran Leadership for this planet and this Region of the Domain, you blurt out your biases and opinions like you were speaking to the workers in your office."

"The Rocara are leaving, and we will be in charge after they leave. So why shouldn't I begin to act in any way I want to?"

"You are getting ahead of things, Ser Lid," Ilanni said. "The Rocara haven't left, and the Administrator has not developed his plans for the transition to self-rule yet. You may not be in the position you envision when he is done."

"But I'm the City Manager!" Amdar said defiantly.

"How did you become City Manager, Ser Lid?" Ilanni asked.

"The Rocara appointed me to the post before you became Planet Manager, Sera Tone, because they thought I was the best qualified among those who applied for the position," Amdar said proudly.

Ilanni smiled knowing that Amdar had just made the point she was raising, even if he didn't see it. Amdar just kept the proud smile on his face as if he had established his right to the position.

After a moment Sam began telling the group about his plans for elections, mining and manufacturing, building a new factory, and establishing a bank.

"Why would we need an election?" Amdar asked indignantly. "All the necessary government positions are filled. Also, we already have a bank in Rotahra. I own it, and we will be glad to issue a loan to build your new factory."

"You just answered your own question, Ser Lid," Sam said. "A government has to have the willing support of the governed, or it will fail. Those who are in the current leadership positions will have the opportunity to submit their candidacy for those positions as part of the elections. We won't need your loan for the factory."

"Who will be permitted to vote in these elections, and if you don't need a loan, why would you need a bank?"

"All the residents in this city and around the planet will be eligible to vote. In fact, I'm thinking of making it mandatory, that everyone votes."

"That doesn't make any sense," Amdar said. "How would the peasants know who to elect or how to run a government?"

"They may know more than you think," Sam said. "What they don't know, they can learn."

"Why bother?"

"Because this is *their* planet, Amdar, every bit as much as it is yours and the other well-to-do Batani."

It was clear that Amdar just couldn't fathom why anyone would take the trouble to ask peasants about government. Apparently, he was going to let that pass, but he was still interested in why Sam would want to set up a bank.

"You didn't answer my question about a bank, Administrator Baxter."

"If the peasants are going to rise above their meager standard of life, they need to have access to credit. I doubt that your bank is lending money to those like Hocan Duar, but it is just those people who need it most."

"Who would lend them money?" Amdar said incredulously. "They don't have the means to pay it back."

"We are planning to help them improve their means," Sam said. "I have explained enough, Ser Lid. I need to meet with Ser Duar and his friends and spend the rest of this visit with Sera Tone and her staff. You will have other opportunities to discuss these matters as they unfold, but for now I must ask you to leave us."

It was obvious that Amdar Lid was not used to being told to leave before he was ready to leave. He didn't know what to do. He sat in his chair fuming until he finally recognized that everyone was looking at him and expecting him to leave the room. He rose in an imperious manner and, strutted out of the room.

"Would you like to meet with Duar and his friends now, Administrator Baxter?" Ilanni asked.

"In a moment, Ilanni," Sam said.

"Janus, I think in the end he will be harmless, but Amdar Lid might cause some mischief. Could you keep watch on him?"

"Yes. I agree with your assessment of Amdar Lid, Sam. I will monitor him."

Sam explained what areas his team would focus on and asked her to introduce them to the Rocara who would be the most helpful to work with. He also told her how informal he was about titles and protocol.

"Since you alerted me to your needs, Sam, I have the right Rocara waiting. We can begin right away."

"Thank you. As you can see by the City Manager's reactions to the plans, there are false assumptions flying through the Batani population which need to be dealt with before they get out of hand. For my next meeting, I will meet with Hocan Duar and friends by myself."

Sam explained his reasoning when he saw the astonished look on Ilanni's face.

"It has nothing to do with you or your staff, Ilanni. I think Ser Duar will be more candid with me if there are no Rocara or other Batani in the room."

Ilanni offered to have the Batani brought to Sam. He said he wanted to go to them. He imagined they were already uncomfortable being in Rocaran Headquarters. It may have been the first time they had ever been in the building. Ilanni led Sam to the room where the Batani were waiting. When Sam entered, all the Batani immediately stood up.

"Please be at ease, Ser and Sera. Have you been treated well while you have waited?"

"Yes, Ser Administrator," Duar said. "Your agreement to meet with us, and in this building, is an unusual experience for us."

"I understand," Sam said, smiling casually. "What I am about to discuss with you will probably fall into that same category."

27. The New Septcium

Sam had learned a great deal in his discussion with Duar. The methods the rich Batani used to keep people like Hocan Duar in their place were harsh. Their methods just strengthened his resolve to make the changes he was planning. It was the local Batani police that carried out some of these abuses. That would be stopped right away. Sam asked the local Rocara to help make the necessary changes. Janus would be watching and would keep Sam informed.

The innate intelligence and clear thinking exhibited by Duar and his friends encouraged Sam. If this was typical among the Batani, they would rapidly adapt to the changes Carmen had outlined. Also, the Batani would have little difficulty learning the advanced tasks associated with the new equipment Travis was planning to put on Eltan.

Sam was telling the others what he had learned from his talk with the Batani when he was contacted by Janus.

"Sam, there is trouble in Tetara."

"The Satran?"

"She is safe for the moment. I found one person who was working on plans to poison her. I had the impression that Garan Ratra might be behind that. I have put the person to sleep and they have been confined, as you suggested the Satran do in such instances."

"What would Garan gain by her death?"

"I don't understand it either," Janus said. *"There is also a small protest outside the Septcium Tower. I am sure that the*

instigators were put up to it by Ratra. I think it would be advisable if you were to go to the Rocaran Capital."

Janus had included Carmen as he discussed the situation with Sam. So she knew why he had paused for a time. Ilanni and Kemel didn't.

"Pardon my lapse," Sam said. "I was thinking about something for a moment. Ilanni, Kemel, I am going to have to leave Eltan. I don't know how long I will be gone. I am leaving Carmen here to work with you. She has the authority to make the necessary decisions. Please excuse me.

He rose from his chair and spoke privately with Carmen as he did.

"Carmen I will be taking Thelika with me. Ask Ahleeto to send one of the other ships here to provide transportation for you and the others."

"Will do." Carmen said. *"Do you need help? You could ask Jesse to accompany you."*

"I hadn't thought of that. You're right. I'll ask him."

"Ilanni, Kemel, thank you for helping my staff. Carmen, I'll contact you later."

With that, Sam headed toward the exit. Sam asked Jesse to join him, and he met Sam at the door. They walked rapidly to where they had parked and took one of the two HSHP's up to Thelika. When they entered the common room Thelika immediately went to Siana and assumed an orbital position above Tetara. They chose to land the HSHP in the plaza outside the Septcium tower, behind the small group that had formed in front of the door.

They left the HSHP and walked toward the group. The Rocara parted to let them through. There were two Rocara on the steps leading up to the door who had been addressing the group. They stopped what they were saying and turned toward Sam and Jesse.

"What do you two want in the tower of the Septcium of the Rocara?" The speaker attempted to speak to them in a disrespectful tone. He needed more practice. To Sam it sounded more like whining. Sam turned to look at the crowd's reaction. They didn't seem impressed either.

"We were on our way to talk with the Satran," Sam said. "We saw you gathered here and wondered what you were discussing."

"Not that it is of any of your concern, but we were discussing the Satran's plan to lead our subjects to self-rule and to return their planets to them."

"It sounds like you are not in favor of the decision. Why not?" Sam asked.

"Several reasons," the protester said.

"Could you name a few, so I can understand your objections?"

"Sure. They are not bright enough to run things for themselves."

"Have you met the Batani?" Sam asked.

"No. I do not need to meet them to know that I am right."

Sam looked at the protester and then to the small group they had been speaking to. "I just came from Eltan, and I am able to confirm that your first objection is wrong. The Batani are very intelligent. Do you have another objection?"

"Those planets are ours. The Rocara have put a great deal of capital into developing operations there. The Satran cannot just give it all away."

"You said just a moment ago that the Satran was planning to 'return their planets to them.' Even you believe that those planets don't belong to the Rocara. To your second point, I am the Administrator for the Tarkan Region. I am planning to negotiate a settlement for the Rocaran investments on the planets, rather than giving it away as you suggest. I believe the

Satran has similar ideas for implementing her plan across the Domain.

"Instead of trying to stir up opposition to the Satran's plan, wouldn't it be better to try to help her succeed in a way that would be good for the Rocara, as well as those they currently rule?"

The protester didn't have an answer to that and looked frustrated because he didn't. The small crowd that had gathered smiled at Sam, and quietly went on their way. Sam and Jesse turned and went into the Septcium tower, leaving the two protesters standing by themselves on the steps.

They went to the Satran's outer office. Aluta said the Satran had been waiting for them and showed Sam and Jesse into the office. The Satran rose from her desk and came around to greet them. Sam introduced Jesse as one of his team helping to manage the business of the Tarkan Region.

"Good to meet you, Jesse. Welcome to Tetara. I wish your first visit could have been under better circumstances."

She turned to Sam.

"Have your 'watchers' informed you of recent events, Sam?"

"Yes, Satran. I would like to meet with the person you have confined. Apparently he was developing a plan to poison you."

The Satran gasped.

"Don't worry. We would never let anything like that happen. My information is that Garan Ratra was behind the small protest I saw on the steps to the building. My watcher has the impression that Administrator Ratra may also be connected to the poisoner and may have helped plan the attack. If I talk to that person, I may be able to learn the truth."

"What could Garan hope to gain?" asked the Satran.

"I've wondered about that myself," Sam said. "Perhaps he is hoping to stop the changes you have announced, or at least delay them. A small amount of chaos at the beginning of implementing something as monumental as you have declared could have a disruptive effect."

"What do you suggest, Sam?"

"I think it would be a good idea to call a Septcium meeting. For those Administrators who are not in the city, I can have Jesse take our ship to pick them up."

"What would be the agenda for such a meeting?" Dahtra asked.

"I suggest that we ask the Administrators to talk about their ideas for implementing your plan in their Regions. I've already begun implementation planning. Perhaps the others have at least started thinking about how to do it. I think such a constructive and positive discussion of something that he apparently opposes, will draw Ratra's opposition out in the open where it can be dealt with."

"You have already started, Sam?" Dahtra asked. "I only made the announcement two days ago."

"Yes, we have begun, and a good thing we have. When I visited Eltan before coming here I learned that rumors were already spreading, and assumptions being made about what your announcement meant for the Batani. They were different than what I had planned. It's probably a good idea to tell you our ideas ahead of the meeting. If I have started something that you don't like, I would rather that we had a chance to discuss it privately, so I can make changes before I go public."

Dahtra asked Aluta about the location of the Administrators and learned that only Cartran Herc needed to be picked up. She told Aluta to announce the Septcium meeting. Jesse left to pick up Cartran, and Sam told Dahtra his plans for Eltan and the Batani. Her only reaction was amazement.

"How do you know how to do these things, Sam?"

"I have been the leader of a large enterprise on my planet for a long time. I have a tremendous staff running it for me. I brought a few members of that staff to Tarka to put the plan together."

Dahtra looked at him.

"If that is true, Sam, what are you doing out here among the stars doing these things for that odd planet Perillian and the Rocaran Domain?"

"There is a great deal of background you would need to understand my answer. If you can wait a bit longer, I will answer your questions."

Dahtra was curious but knew enough about Sam from their brief time together, that he would tell her when he was ready, and not before.

"Of course, but you must know that I am terribly curious."

"I can imagine, and I appreciate your patience."

Sam had purposely left the planet Tarka and the Ortari to the last. It was time to let her know his plans.

"The Ortari wish us to remove Rocaran operations from their planet. The Regional Offices can stay there longer, but the areas of the planet we have disturbed will be cleaned up and returned to their natural state. There is to be no further contact with the planet, at least for the foreseeable future."

"Again, no explanation?" Dahtra asked.

"Not at this time."

Dahtra nodded. Sam left to meet with the poisoner. Dahtra prepared for the Septcium meeting. Just before the meeting, Sam let her know that the poisoner did have a small, but provable link to Administrator Ratra.

* * *

The Septcium meeting began shortly after Cartran Herc arrived. The Administrators were all seated when Dahtra entered. They rose when she came in and sat down after she had taken her seat.

"Thank you for setting aside whatever you were doing and coming to this unscheduled Septcium meeting on such short notice. There are two things I would like to discuss.

"The first item is that I am eager to hear your thoughts about our move to self-rule for our subjects. Administrator Baxter has told me he has begun planning for the Tarkan Region. I was interested what the rest of you thought. Since I know Sam is prepared, I'll ask him to go first.

Sam told the Septcium of his early planning for Eltan, and the other operations in the region.

"I am already hearing rumblings about your visit to Eltan, from some of the leaders among our subjects in the Materan Region," Garan Ratra said. "Are you intending to eliminate the existing government?"

"The Rocara govern the Batani," Sam said. "The Batani have not had their own government for well over a hundred years. The leaders you speak of are people who were appointed by the Rocara, based on what they did for the Rocara, not what they did for the Batani. I plan to have elections to give all Batani a chance to choose how they will be governed. An element I hadn't mentioned is that there exists a bias of the rich Batani against the others. That bias will be removed with elections."

"How do you plan to pay for these improvements?" Jarad Solbe asked. "How will you compensate the Rocara for the loss of the capital facilities on Eltan?"

"I plan to liquidate former Administrator Trace's wealth. That will pay for some of the plan. In addition, it appears that Administrator Trace had been skimming ten percent off the revenue that was supposed to go to the Domain's central treasury. We will eliminate that practice and use those funds to help pay for the changes. I expect to negotiate with the new Batani government to receive compensation for the existing facilities and the improvements."

Sam heard some gasps when he announced the liquidation and the skimming. Before they could protest Sam added a footnote.

"I have only been an Administrator for a few days. After seeing what Trace did in the Tarkan region, I wondered about the role of Administrators. My expectation was that an Administrator was to work for the good of the Rocara by managing their Region efficiently. Trace's apparent goal was to maximize his wealth. I believe the respect for the Septcium would be diminished if the Rocara learned that all Administrators were doing what Trace did."

"Who are you to come in here after 'a few days,' and describe our roles and ridicule past practices of a valued colleague whose life was ended by you?" Garan demanded.

Choosing to ignore the reference to the Tezaxt, Sam said, "Pardon me. I didn't mean to offend. Then the role of an Administrator *is* to maximize his wealth at the expense of the Domain?"

Garan didn't know what to say, and the other Administrators didn't either. Dahtra let the awkwardness hang for a moment before changing the subject by asking what others had thought about self-rule. Cartran Herc and Herata Demis shared their thoughts. Jarad Solbe mumbled something that turned out to be nothing.

Garan Ratra slammed his fist on the table and shouted, "What you have declared for the Rocara people is wrong, Satran. I will not support it."

"I can manage with your lack of support, Garan." Dahtra said. "You can be replaced. What I cannot abide is active opposition. There was a protest that was organized and begun today on the steps of this building. It failed. Apparently no Rocara agreed with the protesters. There was a plot to poison me which was stopped before it could be implemented. Garan, I know you were behind the protest. There is a possible link between you and the Rocaran that was going to poison me. You will bring your resignation to me shortly after this meeting. Also, I suggest that if you want to enjoy your forced, early retirement you will cease this futile opposition!"

28. Pax Rocara

Septcium Tower

The Septcium meeting ended shortly after Dahtra ordered Garan to resign. The next thing she did was to retire Jarad Solbe. She asked Herata, Cartran, Milan and Sam into her office, and began the discussion about creating a new Domain.

"If you are going to facilitate trade among all your former subjects and the Rocara," Sam said, "I suggest that you create a forum for establishing a general agreement about how that trade will take place. Assuming a Trade Federation can be established, how will transactions be handled?"

"I see what you mean." Cartran said. "We buy their goods now. Would that be the same in the future?"

"If you are the purchaser and shipper of all goods, you have all the power," Sam said. "Even if you are completely fair in the way you go about it, things will feel the same to your subjects. You would still have control over them. As we're thinking about this, what currency is used in the Domain?"

"The Rocaran dinal," Dahtra said. "There remain a few cases where there is a local currency, but that is only for local trade."

"Using a single currency across the federation will be even more important now," Sam said. "In the future system a merchant on Eltan might want to buy the goods of a supplier on Xarta, without you being involved in the transaction except to ship the goods from one planet to the other."

"How will they do that?" Herata asked. "How will they know about the goods for sale on another planet? Even if we continue to use the dinal as the currency for the transaction, how will the funds get from the merchant to the supplier?"

After the lively exchange, the long pause after Herata's comment was very noticeable. The four Rocara looked at Sam.

"Sam?" Dahtra asked.

"Huh? Oh, sorry. I was just thinking about Herata's excellent question. I have an idea."

"Can you tell us about it, Sam?" Dahtra asked.

"I'd rather not at this point, Dahtra. I need to check with some of my people to see if it is possible. If it is alright with you, I'd like to leave now to work with them."

Sam decided it was time to talk with Martha who was still aboard Thelika. That's where he went next.

"Martha, how would you like to be an interstellar bank?"

"You brought me along to help on Perillian and didn't use me there. Then you have me sitting here idle while you go about fixing things, and now you surprise me with this idea," Martha said.

"All true, and I'm sorry," Sam said. "This has been unfair to you. I think this idea might make up for it though. I don't even know if it's possible. I thought I'd ask you and Sameer Ahad at Sunaj about it."

"Shall I connect him, now?"

"What do you mean?"

"Sameer has refined the technology that he originally designed to allow Janus and me to communicate telepathically."

There was a pause and then a new voice spoke through Martha.

"Sam, are you there?" Sameer asked. "Martha said you wanted to talk with me."

"Hi, Sameer. I haven't been keeping up with your developments, but Martha says you have improved the design for her to speak telepathically."

"It's true, and it's a good thing I did," Sameer said. "You have placed copies of Martha on other planets you've visited. If it weren't for my technology, you would end up with three completely different versions of Martha, because of their different experiences."

"What do you mean?" Sam asked.

"I'll answer that one, Sameer," Martha said. "With Sameer's new technology, each copy now knows everything the others do. There is only one of me. I just happen to be in several locations at the same time."

"Doesn't that violate some sort of principal?" Sam asked.

"Only if you are an organic being," Martha answered.

"Hmmm," Sam said. "You are a wonder, Martha."

Sam learned that Martha didn't need to be the bank with the new Interstellar Communications Network, or ICN, connecting all of the star systems in the Domain, the banks on each planet could handle the transactions. After a few weeks of working with Rocaran engineers, Sameer had the ICN system ready to go.

"Sameer, I'd like you to set up a station here in my Tarkan office," Sam said, "and then travel with Jesse to set one up at the Satran's office at the Rocaran capital."

Jesse, Sameer and his engineer left right after they set up Sam's ICN station on his desk. About two hours later, a blinking green light on his system indicated he had an incoming call. He answered and saw Dahtra's face on his screen. Sam wasn't sure what to say on this momentous occasion. He opted for something simple.

"Hello, Satran."

* * *

Six months after the creation of the Trade Federation, Sam and the original crew of Humans he had brought to the Rocaran Domain were in the meeting room in the Rocaran Headquarters on Tarka.

"You were right about the Batani," Kristen Rodgers said. "They are bright and have quickly picked up the skills needed to run the bank as well as budgeting of all their government institutions."

"Do you think it would be a good time to leave them on their own, Kristen?" Sam asked.

"Not entirely, but I think it is a good time for us to back away. They may make some mistakes, but they will become stronger as they work their way toward their own solutions."

"That is also true about our involvement in the governments that have been set up on Eltan and other planets," Carmen said. "They have had their elections and have chosen their leaders. We need to get out of their way. I've already started sending our Human volunteers home. They will all be home within a few days."

"Does that mean we will need fewer Lorengi ships?" Ahleeto asked.

"That's possible," Sam said. "How many ships will you need for what you are doing, Travis?

"We won't need quite as many, Ahleeto," Travis answered, "but will continue to need one or two ships to distribute new equipment when it's ready."

"What about the cleanup of the sites on Tarka, Travis?" Sam asked.

"That is complete. We haven't done anything with the offices and living quarters at this site, because they are still in use by our people and the Rocara. As that need is reduced we are planning to take them down, too."

"When you get to that point, check with me," Sam said. "I think we are going to need to leave a few of the buildings in place."

"Why is that, Sam?" Jesse asked. "Are we planning to stay out here?"

"That's the next thing I wanted to talk about.

"Are you with us, Janus?"

"Always, Sam. What do you have in mind?"

"We have accomplished what we set out to do with the Rocara. I think it is time to return to our original investigation. We were brought out here to learn about the possible danger on Perillian. I think there is more to learn. Then there are the Ortari and Merillian, as the Urritan called the planet. The Ortari said there were Urritan artifacts and perhaps the Urritan themselves on this planet. I'd like to find out what that means."

"So would I," Jesse said.

The others expressed their interest as well.

"I will be visiting the Satran today," Sam said. "When I get back we can visit the Ortari settlement and learn where the Urritan may be found."

* * *

Sam took a moment to provide his wife, Lesley with an update on his plans. Then he contacted the Satran ahead of time to make sure she was in her office and had time to see him. She was waiting for him when he arrived.

"Good to see you again, Sam," Dahtra said. "We have both been so busy transforming the Domain we have not met in a while. Even our recent Septcium meetings have been held using the new ICN you gave us. What can I do for you?"

Sam provided an assessment of the progress that had been made to date and told her that many of the humans would be going home.

"Does that mean that you will be leaving us, Sam? I knew you would someday, but I will miss you. You have pacified the

Rocara and the others in the Domain. You created an aura of calm and trust between the Rocara and our former subjects that made the transformation possible. Did you put something in the water?"

Sam laughed at Dahtra's very Human phrase.

"No, nothing in the water," Sam said. "Just as you had recognized that it was time for this change, so did your subjects. You both dreaded the possibility of a violent confrontation. We helped you do it in a peaceful way, which didn't damage the good that was part of the former system.

"You remarked at the time on the symbolism of the Tezaxt, where Rulian forced a showdown. I tried to have a peaceful conclusion to the combat. He forced the issue, and the old ways died with him. That day the Rocara went from overlords to being helpful facilitators."

Sam looked closely at Dahtra who hadn't stirred. There were tears flowing down her cheeks over the tiny green scales.

"Thank you, Sam. In those few insightful words you painted an accurate image of our situation at the time of your arrival. I had not realized how much tension was still in me from having to hold everything together. I can finally let go of it now."

"Your Domain reminded me of another empire on another planet. They had a period of peace and stability about as long as you had since the time of Tablar Ken. At the end of their stable period, a decline began because they tried to hold on to the past. That did not happen here because you were the Satran at this crucial moment in Rocaran history. If you had held on to the old ways, the Rocaran Domain would have embarked on an extended period of decline and violence. You have chosen a different path."

"Again, thank you, Sam. It would have been very difficult to bring this about without you."

"You are welcome. I wanted to let you know that I will be closing the Regional Office on Tarka. Almost everything is being dismantled, and the ground is being restored to a more natural state. It is what the Ortari want. They also want us to stay longer, so I plan to keep some of the buildings. The Ortari do not want anyone else to come to their planet. I think you and the others would be wise to honor that.

"I trust you, Sam. We will honor the wish of the Ortari. Now will you answer one question for me?"

"Of course."

"Why?"

"What do you mean, Dahtra?"

"Why have you, Sam, and the others with you taken all this time out of your lives to help all of us, who were complete strangers to you? Cartran, Herata, Milan and I have wondered about this. You have given us no reason to be suspicious of your motives, but that just makes the reason for your presence all the more mysterious. Why are you here helping us? Surely there are things you could be doing to aid people on your own planet."

Sam thought about the Satran's question. How could he explain that responding to the needs of others was as natural as taking his next breath? It wasn't a creed or a belief, it was deeper than that.

"Our thoughts always are about how we can help. There are many of us on our home planet addressing needs there. Those of us who came here responded to the first request that came from a race on another planet. So we continue to work out here."

"What about your lives and families at home?"

"This is our life. Our families are doing similar things at home. We stay in contact, but we are always focused on what needs to be done. This is who we are. This is what we do."

211

29. Nahnra

Planet Tarka

Sam took his leave from Dahtra and went back to Tarka, and met with Ahleeto, Carmen, Jesse, Kristen, Thornton and Travis at the Headquarters building. They were all still interested in meeting with the Ortari. They packed the HSHP for an extended stay in the forest. They connected with Martha and Thelika, who were in orbit above the Rocaran complex and Janus, to tell them where they were going.

Sam flew the HSHP. He knew the way and it took very little time to arrive at the Ortari village. When they landed, Artis and several other Ortari were there to greet them. Artis seemed excited. They found out why when he spoke.

"They have contacted us!" Artis said, surprising the visitors by using English instead of Rocaran. "The Urritan have connected with the Ortari again. It is because you are here. We are to lead you to the entrance of the underground chamber!"

The team hoisted their day packs onto their shoulders and followed Artis and the others to the Ortari village. When Sam had visited the village before, all of the Ortari were quiet and calm. Not this time! Every Ortari was in the center plaza talking and moving about, as excited as Artis.

"How did the Urritan contact you?" Jesse asked Artis. "After all this time how could they even be alive?"

"I was going to ask the same question, Jesse," Ahleeto said. "I'm not sure that the Lorengi digital storage technology will keep me functioning that long."

"We received the message in here," Artis said, pointing to his head. "We were to lead you to the entrance when you arrived. It was not known when that would be. We were to prepare. As you can see looking around at the activity, we are ready."

"Let's not make you wait any longer," Carmen said. "Please take us there."

Artis led them further into the forest. The entire village followed after them. On the last part of the journey they had to pass through a growth of trees that was so dense they sometimes had to turn sideways to get between the trunks. The trunks had smooth bark and were uniformly two feet in diameter.

After moving through thirty feet of trees they came upon a circular clearing about fifty feet in diameter. The foliage of the surrounding trees, which started about twenty feet above the ground, left only a small opening for the sunlight to come through. There was enough light to see that the ground was covered with of thick moss, and to see the moss-covered mound in the center.

The mound was twenty feet high and thirty feet across. The entrance in the side of the mound was surrounded by a twelve-inch-thick rope-like frame, made of woven bronze-colored metal of some kind. Although there was dust on the metal, it had been kept free of the surrounding forest growth that had claimed the rest of the mound and showed no sign of age. The ornate door within the frame was fifteen feet high and four feet wide. It was made of the same metal, and had many fascinating designs etched into its face. It also showed no signs of age.

"It's beautiful, Artis," Carmen said. "It looks like it must have on the day it was put in place."

"Thank you, Carmen. The Urritan made the entrance, but we take pride in cleaning it, and keeping the forest away from it," Artis said.

"I had been wondering why the Rocara had not come upon the entrance when you first told me of it, Artis," Sam said. "Now I understand. This clearing and mound would have been hidden from view by the thick growth of trees. They would have had no reason to squeeze through the trees as we did, but they might have detected the metal from orbit. I wonder...

"Thelika, can you detect any metal where we are standing?" Sam asked, using his implant.

"No, I cannot Sam," Thelika answered, including the rest of the team through their implants. "I can detect a very small temperature variation from the surrounding area. It's a bit warmer below where you are standing. It is so small a difference that I wouldn't have noticed it in my typical survey of a planet."

"Thanks, Thelika." Sam said. "So the Urritan used the passive devices of the trees, metal that can't be detected, and masking most of the heat they generate below to avoid detection. We'll have to see if they have any active defenses that might be employed if someone finds them in spite of the care they've obviously taken. Hopefully we won't trigger them, since we've been invited."

"How do we get in?" Jesse asked. "I don't see a doorknob."

"Artis, did you get instructions on how to open the door?" Carmen asked.

"The message said that when you were ready, the door would open for you," Artis, said with excitement. "The message also said that we could come in with you."

There was a whisper of a sound coming from the direction of the door. Everyone looked in time to see the door slide silently to the right. They went toward the entrance and looked in. They saw a metal ramp that sloped downward through a passage, which was lit by a soft green light emanating from the walls.

"Looks like we have been invited in," Sam said. "Let's go meet our hosts."

The passage was wide enough that the Humans and Ahleeto could have walked abreast of each other but chose to organize themselves in two rows. Artis and the other Ortari followed behind them.

"I'm glad they used a ramp," Jesse said, as they walked down the passage. "If the Urritan were as big as we think they were, stairs to fit them might be a bit awkward for us."

The passage was dark in the distance but as they walked the walls continued to light up to illuminate their way. They had walked down the ramp for five minutes when it turned sharply to the right. In another five minutes, it turned to the right again. They spiraled down the ramp this way for twenty minutes. When they came to the bottom, the walls of an enormous room lit up before them. The room was one-hundred feet across and covered by a domed metal ceiling which was thirty feet tall at the center.

There was equipment in the room that was all made of the same bronze-colored metal as entrance. The visitors walked into the room and looked around. There were lights on some equipment panels, and a soft hum could be heard in the room. The panel lights were mostly blue or green, and all were dim. There was one larger light on one of the panels which was orange colored and brighter than the rest. It was blinking as if to alert the operator.

"Artis, do you know what the equipment in this room was used for?" Sam asked.

Artis looked like he was struggling to answer Sam's question when a bass-toned voice spoke into the room.

"It is alright, Artis. I will answer Sam's question. First let me introduce myself. I am Nahnra."

The visitors looked around to see the origin of the voice. They didn't see an obvious source.

"The Ortari were never told the purpose of anything in this facility," Nahnra said. "They were companions and were very important to the Urritan in that role. Since the Urritan ceased to exist, the Ortari have been relegated to maintaining the outside of this facility."

"The Ortari have remarkable minds," Sam said. "I've enjoyed the time I've spent with Artis and the others. Their ability to sense the universe is amazing."

"Yes they do have fine minds," Nahnra said.

"Could you tell us about yourself, Nahnra?" Carmen asked.

"I am the digital embodiment of all that was the Urritan race," Nahnra said. "To answer Sam's earlier question, this is the control room for the entire facility, which stretches a great distance in all directions below the surface. The facility's purpose is to support the continuation of the essence of the Urritan, in other words, me, and to store artifacts they thought were important."

Carmen had expected to find individual stored personalities, similar to the form the Lorengi had chosen. She wondered what became of the Urritan. Had they loaded what they were and knew into a database to become part of the "digital embodiment" of their race, and then died, or "cease to exist" as Nahnra had said. She chose to be patient and see if her questions would be answered as they learned more from Nahnra.

30. For Whom the Light Shines

Planet Tarka (Merillian), in the Urritan Chamber

The Ortari walked around the control room, looking at equipment they hadn't seen for a very long time, and talking in hushed tones. They raised their voices occasionally when one or another recognized something that had been important to them when they served the Urritan. Travis and Thorton, the team's engineers, also began exploring.

"Have you recently been in contact with the intelligence on the planet we first visited?" Jesse asked. "It called itself Agar, in our language."

"Yes, Jesse," Nahnra said. "Before your arrival at Perillian, a different ship visited that planet. Agar sent me a message describing the event. It said that the ship probed the planet, and then quickly went away. Agar did not know what to make of it. Did you learn why the ship left quickly?"

"To answer that question, Nahnra," Sam said, "I will need to introduce another of our party, Janus. While I'm at it I should also introduce our team including the Lorengi, Ahleeto and the Lorengi ship, Thelika, and aboard Thelika, is cyber intelligence like you, named Martha."

Sam told Nahnra about each individual he mentioned and their area of expertise.

"What an interesting array of sentients," Nahnra said. "Ahleeto, we'll have to compare notes on the way your people and mine chose to extend themselves digitally."

Nahnra paused for a moment.

"I have established a communications link with the Lorengi ship. Thelika and Martha, perhaps we could begin exchanging data, to broaden our understanding of each other."

Sam received confirmation that the link was functioning from Martha, through his implant.

"Sam, how may I communicate with Janus?" Nahnra asked.

"Interesting question," Sam said. "Let's see. Martha can communicate with Janus telepathically. Martha can communicate with you digitally through the communications link you now have established. Yes, I think that will work. Martha, can you set up a path through you so that Janus can communicate with Nahnra."

"I did it as soon as you suggested it, Sam," Martha said.

"Hello, Nahnra," Janus said to Nahnra through Martha, and to those in the room through their implants so everyone was in on the conversation. "I think we have many things to talk about."

Sam agreed with Nahnra. It was an "interesting array of sentients." Now they were all communicating with each other. He could imagine that Thelika, Martha and Nahnra were doing so at phenomenal speeds while still being able to keep up with the conversations in the Urritan chamber.

"Janus, could you tell me what you sensed about the planet?" Nahnra asked.

"I did not sense thoughts, but I could detect very strong feelings. In our time with the Rocara, we confirmed that the crew of the Rocaran ship did get a very strong feeling that they were not welcome. The planet responded that way because it sensed that the Rocara were intending to mine the surface and cut down the Teratta."

"Why did you go to the planet?" Nahnra asked. "From what I have learned already, it is located a long way from your home world."

"I received a message urging us to go to Perillian," Janus said. "I had been receiving messages from this source for a short while. The other messages were only conveying information, which the sender seemed to think would be useful for me. Then I receive the urgent request."

"Did the source say why?" Nahnra asked.

"No. We first believed that we were called to help protect the unique emerging sentience that the planet was becoming. That may have been the major reason. Then we became involved with the Rocara and helped them find a solution to a situation that might have become violent. Now in this same part of the Galaxy, we also are learning about the Urritan. Perhaps we were called because of all of this, to help where we could and learn what we can."

"Who sent the message in the first place?" Nahnra asked.

"We don't know," Sam said. "When we got to the planet, we thought it might have been the planet that sent for help. When we learned of you, we thought it might have been you."

"Me?" Nahnra asked. "How would I even know of you? You are so far away from here. How would I even conceive of a being like you, Janus?"

"I understand," Janus said. "As soon as I became aware of you, I knew it wasn't you."

"Then who did send the message?"

"We do not know."

"Have you received any messages since your arrival?"

"No," Janus said. "I have not received a message after the one urging us to come to Perillian."

Sam had wondered about that. Who was this other Entity? Was it done with them now that they had completed what needed to be done here? Would Janus get more messages? It would serve no purpose to think about it now, and there was plenty of mystery to be explored in this chamber.

"We probably will not know more unless Janus receives another message," Sam said. "For now, I am wondering why you wanted us to come to your chamber. Was it just to thank us for protecting Perillian from the Rocara?"

"Since Perillian is one of the Urritan works, I do thank you, but that is not the reason. I was eager for you to enter the chamber because you are the race the Urritan had in mind to receive all they had to offer, all that is stored here."

"Us?" Sam asked. "How could the Urritan know of us? If I understand the timing correctly, they ceased to exist, as you put it, about two million years ago. As we understand our history, the hominids we descended from might not have even existed then."

"I cannot be sure they knew of you specifically, but I would not be surprised if they did somehow," Nahnra said. "They told me that a race would come in the future that would be of such a nature as to be worthy to receive what they had to offer. I was to expect such an arrival. I was to give those who came my complete support, all the information that is in me, and everything else the Urritan chose to place in this enormous facility. Everything that is within this chamber, including me is to be yours to use in any way you see fit."

"Why?" Sam asked. "Why did they give you those instructions?"

"They were dying," Nahnra said. "They were a race that had existed for five-hundred thousand years. During that time, right up to the end, they sought to help others and all forms of life in their struggle to survive. They wanted to support those who would do the same when they arrived at some point in the distant future."

"We are honored that you think we are that race," Carmen said. "What makes you think that we are the ones the Urritan said would be coming?"

"You see that orange light blinking on one of my panels?" Nahnra asked.

"Yes," Carmen said.

"I have been watching that light for two million years," Nahnra said. "I was told that it would light up and begin to blink when the right people arrived. Over that time, many have flown by. Some have even landed on the surface as the Rocara did. Nothing that has happened caused it to light up until now. It started blinking the day you arrived on Perillian."

The chamber had returned to the almost total silence that was present when they first arrived. The only sound was the soft hum of machinery. The Ortari had stopped talking among themselves. The Humans and Ahleeto were too stunned to speak.

Sam thought about what Nahnra had said. The AI was certain that they were the ones who were to inherit the legacy of the Urritan. That belief was based on the blinking of an orange light on the panel. What could the Urritan have been seeking, which if found would have then triggered the light?

In recent years Sam had witnessed many things which his early education and experience would have labeled as impossible. After having witnessed them, Sam had to adjust his criteria for the use of that word. Now this! An apparently very powerful and advanced civilization had set up this AI to wait for a race that would have something which would cause the orange light to blink, and that race would inherit all the Urritan had left. Amazing!

"Couldn't it just be a malfunction?" Jesse asked. "Perhaps after all this time you are misremembering what it is for, and the orange light just indicates that there is something wrong in your system."

"No, Jesse," Nahnra said. "The Urritan did not have malfunctions, and my memory is accurate. The light is blinking for the reason I stated, and your presence is the cause."

"Do you know what we did or what there is about us that could cause the light to blink?" Carmen asked.

The Ortari had silently gathered around the Humans. This time it was Artis who answered for Nahnra.

"Nahnra does not know the answer, Carmen. The Ortari do." Artis said.

All eyes turned to Artis.

"What do you mean, Artis?" Nahnra asked, a bit indignantly. "I know everything the Urritan knew and did."

"Not this, Artis said. "This was only shared between the Urritan and the Ortari. You said that we were valuable as companions to the Urritan. We were that, but we were also something more, something which they had not expected when they cloned us. We have what Sam spoke of—a very close connection to the universe. It was that which the Urritan found so valuable in our companionship. Through us they could better understand the universe and themselves.

"We were able to show that what they were and did in the physical world and their effect on the energy of universe were reflections of each other. It was that which they sought in another race. They told us that when we detected others which had a similar effect on the universe we were to send a certain mental signal to a particular section of the systems below.

"We had not encountered an image like the Urritan's for a long time. Then we detected the Humans arrival at Perillian. We sensed that they had what the Urritan were looking for and sent the signal. Apparently that started the light blinking."

31. Chamber of Wonders

Planet Tarka (Merillian), in the Urritan Chamber

Silence filled the chamber again.

Sam was beginning to think that it might be true. The Humans and the collective consciousness of Earth, Janus, might be who the Urritan race were looking for. So what did being the heirs of the Urritan mean? The answer to that question might elude them for a while. What should they do next? Jesse answered the question.

"I'm not sure what all this means," Jesse said, "but perhaps we could take a look at what we apparently have inherited. Where would you suggest we start, Nahnra?"

Nahnra didn't answer right away, perhaps still mulling over having been left out of a key facet of the Urritan race.

"Pardon the delay, Jesse," Nahnra said. "I have what you would call a catalog, but even that is enormous. Perhaps the best way to begin is to give you a tour of the facility."

"How big is this facility?" Travis asked.

"Using your system of measurement we received from Martha," Nahnra answered, "the Chamber is about two-hundred twenty acres, including the space for the two remaining Urritan ships."

"How did they move around in such a large facility?" Carmen asked.

"Even though the Urritan could teleport, as I understand you can, they needed carts at the beginning. Those are available to you. Once you become more familiar with the Chamber you may teleport, but the carts are probably the best way to see the facility for your first time."

Near the back of the chamber a panel ten feet wide and fifteen feet high slid into the wall exposing a passageway that sloped downward. The walls lit up with the same green tinted light as was at the entrance.

There was a room on the right that contained ten flat carts, which were twelve feet long and six feet wide. They had short sides enclosing a seating area, with openings on each side to allow passengers to enter, and a clear, rounded, four-foot-high windshield at each end. They hovered in place about eight inches above the floor.

Sam walked over to where the carts were and pushed on the side of the closest one. It did not move. He noticed that the seats had already been shaped to fit Humans or Ortari.

Sam looked back toward the control room. The Ortari were waiting uncertainly at the entrance to the passageway.

"Artis do you and the others wish to travel along with us?" Sam asked.

Artis and the other Ortari nodded eagerly but did not move.

"Nahnra, is there anything prohibiting the Ortari from coming along in the carts?" Sam asked.

"When the Urritan were here, the Ortari did not go beyond the control room. They were not needed anywhere else. This is your facility now. You may decide where the Ortari go."

"How are these carts operated?"

"I control them, Sam. You merely have to mention the destination and your readiness to leave, and the cart will take you there."

"Since we don't know anything about the place, will you be our guide, Nahnra?" Carmen asked.

"I have planned a tour with stops at several important rooms. I will direct the carts there and will provide the description of what each room contains."

"Your plan sounds like a good one," Sam said. He turned to the Ortari. "The Ortari who want to come along should step into the carts nearest the passage. Artis, I would like it if you would ride with me and my team."

Artis beamed and entered Sam's cart. The rest of the Ortari climbed into nearby carts.

"It looks like we're ready to travel, Nahnra." Sam said.

"I will be with you at your first stop," Nahnra said.

The carts moved out of the room and one-by-one began to travel down the passageway. No noise was created by moving except wind rushing past the front windshield. That noise increased as the speed of the carts rapidly grew to what Sam guessed to be about sixty miles per hour. No sensation of motion could be felt as the cart accelerated, which provided a strange feeling when contrasted to the walls whisking by so rapidly. Sam thought that there must be an inertia-dampening field set up between the two windshields. The same lack of sensation was present when the carts slowed to a stop.

Their first stop was by an opening in the wall of the passage. It was fifteen feet high and ten feet wide, which seemed to be the standard opening size for the Urritan.

As Travis was exiting the cart, he asked, "What powers these carts? How are they suspended above the floor?"

"Gravity fields," Nahnra answered. "All drive mechanisms of the Urritan technology are based on the ability to control gravity."

"How can they still be operational after all this time?" Ahleeto asked. "We Lorengi built things to last, but this time span exceeds anything our designers would have conceived of."

"After their first hundred-thousand years of civilization, the Urritan decided that they would build things that did not wear out. This saved them time and effort as well as resources. Having no moving parts was an important design criterion that was used wherever possible. The bronze-colored metal you see used everywhere is called Altren. It is impervious to most environments and the passage of time. The result is mechanisms that run far into the future. Including those things you will find in this Chamber."

When Nahnra finished speaking the group turned to the room before them. There was no door, but there was a semi-transparent energy field at the opening. There was just enough opacity to allow one to see that it was there. Sam and the others stepped out of their carts and approached the opening. When they were close enough to touch it, the energy field disappeared.

They entered the room filled with kiosks and display cases. It had about four times the floor space as the control room, with the same tall domed ceiling.

"You might call this room the Museum of Planets and Races," Nahnra said. "It contains information and artifacts from all of the planets and races the Urritan encountered in their long sojourn as a race. Take as long as you want to explore each location we visit on the tour, but to thoroughly view everything in this room would take days. I suggest you gather at one of the displays to see a sample of what is here and then move on to the next site."

"I don't know what else is in this wondrous Chamber," Carmen said, "but I know I will be spending most of my time in this room after we get settled."

Sam and Jesse looked at each other, smiling knowingly at Carmen's remark. She walked toward one of the displays and everyone followed. They let the Ortari crowd around Carmen, since the Humans could see the display over them.

Carmen asked Nahnra, "How do I start the display?"

As soon as Carmen finished her question, a high-resolution holographic display began showing a rural setting on some planet with a sun that gave off a slightly red light. At the same time a vocal narrative in English began explaining what was being shown. The view passed over countryside until it came to a small village with huts in a circle around a central clearing.

The villagers walked on four legs, with the front part of their bodies rising up with two arms extending from their shoulders. The horizontal part of their bodies was covered with a large golden shell that was split down the center, while the up-rising part of their bodies and arms were covered with a dark green leathery skin. They appeared to be about five feet tall at the shoulder though it was difficult to gauge without some familiar object to make a comparison.

The narrator explained that the people called themselves Nulfla and provided the name of the planet. The narrator described what was in the adjoining display case and was about to go into more detail when Nahnra interrupted.

"You picked a wonderful example, Carmen," Nahnra said. "The Nulfla are a gentle, agrarian race that the Urritan visited several times. The Nulfla were generous in giving their artifacts. When the Urritan offered gifts in return, they would only accept a few bright objects that they took to be art and put them on display. Everything else was gracefully refused because it had no use for them and would only be in their way."

Carmen was happy to get additional information about the race she had just seen but took Nahnra's hint that it was time to move on. Everyone stepped into the carts and set off to the next stop.

They continued their travels seeing one marvelous room after another, including a room that contained medical equipment that was tailored to the various races the Urritan had encountered. Nahnra explained that the Urritan prepared themselves in case they came upon an emergency situation during their travels. Another room contained an enormous collection of Urritan art as well as that from other races.

At one stop, Nahnra said, "In this room the Urritan stored examples of technological devices. You will find additional examples in other parts of the Chamber, but most of what would interest you will be found in this room. Each display has visual and audio support to show you what the device is used for, how it operates, and the technology behind it."

Travis and Thornton stood up and exited the cart immediately following Nahnra's description and went into the room, not waiting for the others.

Sam smiled and looked at the others who hadn't exited yet.

"Perhaps we'll let the engineers look this one over while the rest of us move on."

Travis looked back over his shoulder and said, "Uh, right, if that's okay."

The rest Sam's team nodded their heads in agreement, and Sam said, "It's fine. We'll check with you later."

Sam would come back to this room but wanted to see the rest of what was stored in the Chamber before he did. The part of the Chamber where they stopped next was different. It had an opening with an energy barrier over it like the others, but in addition there were five large windows of about the same size.

They stepped out of the carts to peer through the windows and saw an enormous cavern. It was over two-thousand feet long, and a thousand-feet wide. The bottom of the cavern was eight-hundred feet below them. The ceiling of the cavern was two hundred feet above where they were standing. There were buildings and scaffolding along the sides of the cavern. Hovering in the middle with no visible support was a ship that nearly filled the cavern.

The ship was made of Altren and was ellipsoidal in shape. There were large, curved windows of different sizes and shapes at each end of the ship, all framed by Altren. A dim light could be seen coming from inside the ship, which provided a limited view of the interior.

When his fascination with the ship subsided and he was able to speak, Jesse asked, "One of the Urritan ships?"

"Yes," Nahnra said. "The other one is in a cavern of similar size just beyond the far wall of this cavern."

"It looks like the ship is made of the same bronze-colored metal that the entrance and much of this chamber is made of," Sam said. "You called it Altren, Nahnra. What is it made of?"

"It's a composite," Nahnra said. "It's more ceramic than metal, although certain metallic ores are used in its manufacture."

"That probably explains why we couldn't detect it as a metal from above the surface," Sam said.

"Yes," Nahnra answered. "Altren has a number of useful properties, which make it a material suitable in all areas of fabrication. The Urritan used it in many applications. Some were larger than the ship you see before you."

"Impressive ship," Jesse said. "It doesn't look like it is supported by anything. Is that the gravity field you mentioned? How does it work?"

"It is complicated," Nahnra answered. "There are technological files that will provide details for you. From the data that we have received from Thelika and Martha, I understand that you have not discovered how to generate gravity.

"I also understand that the Lorengi ships teleport you across vast distances instantaneously. The Urritan ships will get you to places nearly as fast, though the mathematics of navigation are more complicated. Since that is all handled by the shipboard intelligence, you will see little difference when using the Urritan ships. I imagine that you will find other uses for gravity generators as well. The Urritan certainly did."

"Whether we need your ships for travel or not, they are magnificent," Sam said. "I will want to go inside, and if possible travel in them."

"They were the most advanced faster-than-light ships of their time," Nahnra said. "They might still be. I have always liked looking at them from the outside. I thought that the designers were artful when they created them. They are functional, but beautiful at the same time."

"This looks like another exhibit that would take quite a while to view thoroughly," Carmen said. "Do you want to tour the ship now, Sam?"

Sam was obviously torn between wanting to look more closely at the ships and finishing the tour.

"What is left on your guided tour, Nahnra?" Sam asked.

"The key stops that are left are the power plant that provides energy for all operations in the Chamber, and the living quarters and eating area. The last two are being refitted to match your size and needs. The power plant is available for viewing at this time."

"What is the power plant like?" Jesse asked.

"It is a large array of coils underneath a layer of Altren. Below the coils are fluctuating gravity fields which induce an electric current in the coils to provide power for the facility. There are no moving parts, but there is a pulsating hum that can be heard in the large room."

"I would like to learn more about the power plant, the ships, and of the many uses of gravity generators," Sam said, "but I think we are at a point where we should stop and consider what we have already seen.

32. A Limited Venture

In the Urritan Chamber near the ship

"Nahnra, I am having trouble believing that all of this is being passed on to us," Sam said. "You say it is, so I am going to act as if it is true."

Turning to the others, he said, "That means we need to decide what to do with our inheritance. It is a great boon, but it is also a great responsibility."

They rode the carts back to the control room picking up Travis and Thornton on the way. Nahnra led them to a conference room near the control room, and the Ortari went back to their village.

The long table in the center of the conference room was made of Altren. Nahnra had adjusted the room, so the table and chairs fit the Humans.

Once they were all seated, Sam asked, "So we have inherited unknown riches and untold number of technical marvels. What should we do? What about the technology?"

"Is there a problem introducing this technology on Earth?" Carmen asked.

"Although it's a bit of a twist on the usual first-contact scenario," Travis said, "we would be introducing advanced technology into a more primitive culture. Like thoughtful extraterrestrials, we have to be careful about which technologies we introduce, and how fast we introduce them."

His comment caused them all to pause as they tried to wrap their minds around the role reversal Travis had just described.

"Assuming we could choose a technology that could be introduced, how would we do it?" Jesse asked.

"I agree with Travis," Sam said, "and I think I have the answer to your question, Jesse. Sunaj has been introducing new technology for over twenty years now. We could study the chosen technology at Sunaj and decide how to shape the introduction, so it works on Earth."

"What about that this chamber exists, and that Humans have inherited it?" Ahleeto asked. "What do we tell those on Earth? What can I tell my people?"

Sam hadn't thought about the Lorengi when he was considering information management. He had only thought about what to do about Earth.

"We have already brought a number of H2s to work on Rocaran facilities," Sam said. "Our previous contact with other races provides enough for Earth to deal with. We can continue to come to this planet under the guise that it is part of the Rocaran civilization we need to continue to address.

"I think it is too early to tell Earth about the Urritan and what we have inherited. We can use what we have here to aid us if we are called to another part of the galaxy. We will consider the guidelines that Travis raised about what to introduce to our culture. Ahleeto, I think it is alright to talk to the Lorengi about this place and what it contains."

"I agree with you, Sam," Carmen said. "I would love to discuss this with the Lorengi, but I don't think we can share it on Earth yet. Janus what do you think is the right thing to do?"

"I agree with what is being said," Janus said through everyone's implants. "I think telling our world what we have here would have a serious destabilizing effect.

"You haven't discussed what to do about those on Earth who would like to travel to the other planets we have already contacted. Some would like to study them, or to visit as tourists. Unfortunately, many would try to exploit them.

"H2s, and only a small number of them, have been connected to all of this," Janus continued. "H2s move about in Lorengi ships. Are those ships available to H1 Humans? Talk about this has already surfaced among H1s who resent H2s."

Sam had never imagined himself to be in this position. He and a few others now had access to amazing wealth and technology. They were able to travel to other planets and meet new beings. He was now in the position of deciding who would have access to what.

In his heart he wished everyone on Earth could experience this, but in his mind he knew that not everyone should be permitted to. Some would do tremendous damage were they allowed access to what was beyond Earth. It was absolutely against everything he believed in to limit the activities of others, but he would not allow them to harm other races or other planets.

"Ahleeto, will your people agree to limit the use of the Lorengi ships as they have thus far?" Sam asked. "Will they want to let others use them?"

"We will only let those you authorize to use the ships, Sam," Ahleeto said.

"Thank you," Sam said. "As exciting as all of this is, are we in agreement that for now this will have to be a limited venture?"

Sam sounded very business-like, but he was genuinely overwhelmed with the Urritan Legacy. Sam and his team would make good use of what the Legacy provided to help others. What was in the chamber also might help them understand the Urritan, and why they chose him and his companions.

Even though he had just labeled this a "limited venture," Sam was beginning to have visions of a limitless, uncharted future roaming among the stars.

Epilogue

The meeting broke up shortly after Sam and his team agreed to be extremely careful about what of the Legacy they would share with others. Everyone wanted to stay and continue exploring the Chamber. Sam felt the need to connect with his wife. She was not only a wise and understanding person. She was also a U.S. Senator at the forefront of the issues of a growing H2 population on Earth.

"Lesley, I have no way of knowing what time it is there. Can we talk about something?"

"Of course, Sam. I'm on the deck in La Jolla. It's Sunday afternoon. I've been missing you. This would be a great time to talk."

"I'll be right there," Sam said.

Sam contacted Thelika and asked for a ride back to Earth. Once they arrived, Sam teleported to the surface.

The next thing he experienced was that his feet were on wet sand, a gentle, salty breeze was blowing his hair, and he was looking out to sea.

"Are you lost, sailor?" Lesley asked, from the deck behind him. After getting the message from Sam, Lesley thought she should be ready for what "I'll be right there," meant.

Sam remembered the first time Lesley had called him "sailor." It was the morning after their first night together. They had spent it in this same house. He had risen before her that morning. He wanted to take a walk on the beach to think about what their night together meant.

They were just getting used to telepathy. Lesley had risen and begun to get breakfast ready. Not knowing if he had left she had sent, *"Your ship leave port already, sailor?"*

They had been together ever since. Her work was in California and Washington, D. C.. Sam was headquartered in Seattle, but his work took him all over. So theirs had been a long-distance relationship from the beginning. Recently, the "distance" had grown much larger.

Sam turned, looked up at Lesley and answered, "No, Ma'am. Request permission to come aboard." He walked up the stairs leading to the deck. He stopped at the top of the stairs and saluted.

"Permission granted," Lesley said, smiling. "Any tales to share from your travels?"

He walked over to her, reached out, and pulled her close. "Yes, I do."

When they stepped back she motioned to one of the deck chairs and went inside. She came back a few minutes later with a tray of cheese, crackers, fruit, two glasses and a bottle of chilled white wine.

"Ah, the California snack tray," Sam said.

She poured the wine, gave him a glass, sat down, and waited for Sam to tell her what was on his mind.

"Something has come up that I need to talk with you about," Sam said. "What I've been doing recently may cause you trouble."

Lesley smiled. "Sam, you have always stirred things up. It's a natural part of you being a leader in the vanguard of the H2s."

"There's a new dimension to my activities," Sam said. He told her about the Urritan Legacy and their decision to keep it secret. He also mentioned that he and the team thought it was a good idea to be careful who they included in space exploration.

"We have encountered advanced technology that needs to be slowly and carefully introduced to Earth."

"That's not what you are most worried about is it?" Lesley asked, looking at him intently.

"No," Sam said quietly. "I'm mostly concerned about unleashing the unsavory behaviors of Humans on the galaxy."

Lesley paused to consider how this new development would affect the work she was doing to help society adjust to the growing H2 population.

"It's okay, Sam," she said. "It's a good decision, and you have to be the one to make it. It's been that way from the first time we went off-planet. To begin with, it looked like what it was—a scientific venture. As it has expanded, I have heard the rumors that Janus told you about. There are some who see this as something H2s are keeping from H1s. The clamor will get noisier, but it's still the right thing to do.

"You've said that you will introduce some new technology through Sunaj. That will obscure the connection to off-planet sources for most people, and they'll be glad for the new devices. Others will catch on and demand the right of access to it all. It is very much like what you said Travis had characterized it as—a first-contact type of situation."

"Thank you, Lesley. I trust your judgment and am pleased that you see it the same way that I do."

Sam looked down at the glass of wine he had been holding. He hadn't taken a sip, so intent has his attention been on Lesley as she was offering her perspective. He sighed and raised his glass to his lips. He didn't know how long it would last, but it was a relief to be home!

* * *

"Hello," Janus said. He wasn't sure of the nature, name, or anything else about the Entity that he had been calling his "new friend." He tried to concentrate on the nature of his feelings when he received messages in the past. He thought

that they might help him understand the essence of who had been contacting him. Janus had been trying to make the connection for some time now.

"Hello," Janus said again.

"Yes."

Janus was startled when he finally received a response. It was the same Entity, the source of the other messages. The Entity was unlike any other intelligence Janus had encountered—enormous beyond belief and insubstantial to the point of non-existence.

"My fellow travelers and I have questions." Janus said.

"Yes."

"The journey you sent us on had many facets."

"Yes."

"Were all those we encountered, envisioned by you when you sent us there?"

"Yes."

"Did they unfold as anticipated?"

"Better."

That was a qualitative response. It was a good one, but surprising to Janus.

"Are we done?" Janus asked.

"No."

What did that brief answer mean? Janus thought that he might be getting close to finding out. Then just as mysteriously as it had arrived the Entity was suddenly gone!

Be sure to look for the other books in the

Janus Unfolding Series

Emergence
Factotum
Inheritance
Ancient Agendas
The Urritan Legacy

<u>Reviews Matter!</u>

I would appreciate your thoughts about my book. Please
write a review and post it
at
Amazon

C.A. Knutsen was born in the Pacific Northwest with its mountains, rivers and rugged ocean coast. Enjoying the natural beauty, he is especially drawn to the shores of Puget Sound with its majestic, rocky bluffs and forests. This setting inspires his speculations about the wonderful life on this planet and its possible transformations in the future, as well as the role Human beings have in sustaining life and caring for each other.

Knutsen has a Bachelor of Science in Electrical Engineering and a Masters in Business Administration from the University of Washington. His background in science and business, as well as his passion for the environment, now inform his visionary fiction.

caknutsen.com

www.ingramcontent.com/pod-product-compliance
Lightning Source LLC
Chambersburg PA
CBHW032036240626
47154CB00003B/941